A roundtable, unanimous dreamers chime in

Brenda Iijima
&
Janice Lee

meekling press 2023

Meekling Press
Chicago, IL
meeklingpress.com

Printed in the USA.

Cover art by Christine Shan Shan Hou,
"two egrets touching each other, tenderly,"
collage on paper, 2020

ISBN 978-1-950987-28-3

Library of Congress Control Number: 2022949894

“She was sixteen. She had glossy leaves and bursting buds and she wanted to struggle with life but it seemed to elude her.”
—Zora Neale Hurston, *Their Eyes Were Watching God*

“HEY
C’MON
COME OUT

WHEREVER YOU ARE

WE NEED TO HAVE THIS MEETING
AT THIS TREE

AIN’ EVEN BEEN
PLANTED
YET”
—June Jordan, *Calling on All Silent Minorities*

“If someone touches me, I am brought back to my bodily and terrestrial existence, with sometimes an additional aquatic perception, particularly if I am touched through words.”
—Luce Irigaray, *Through Vegetal Being*

“The world is not about to end; we are already living with a different World.”
—Bayo Akomaolafe

“Fire in Squirrels for the Trees in Sun on Earth”
—Unanimous dreamers

FIRE

I was in a rush, crouched over, on my bike, cycling into town when it dawned on me that the shadows were off. As I refocused, I saw that all the trees and the understory of the trees along the route I traveled had been razed on one side of the roadway. All that remained was the stubble of dead growth—the trunks and crowns had been removed and a strong light shone on dry dirt and debris. The denudedness went on like this for miles. There was hardly any traffic so I could glide along, looking at the fallout of the destruction, and wonder out loud what had happened and why it had happened and ponder as to how much of the floral growth along the thoroughfare had been sacrificed.

The sun felt ferocious, its radiant tentacles like sharp swords slashing at my skin, but probably this was my own myopic personification of that star; the sun didn't have an opinion of my existence and it definitely wasn't targeting its attacks on me. I continued mobilizing, parched by the glare of solar radiation and desert-like heat. What I didn't notice were the white airborne follicles lunging in the wind—various seeds and cones of different weights, shapes, and densities.

Seed 1: ...
Seed 2: // .
Seed 3: /. /. /. /////.

And also,
Goose: (wings spreading, wings folding)

The whole of life as somehow constrained through only a few

channels, then refocusing and widening the apertures. The leaves have known such radical permeability all along. And all the world contained in a seed, all that knowledge, which is growth, which is atmosphere, which is breath, which is flight, which is the cosmos, which is the origin of the world.

As if waking up, I disembarked from my bike and stood beside it for a moment, my limbs shaking—I was covered in light, powdery dust-pollen; every hair on my forearms was fluffy with airy, downy material that clung to my body, clung to the electrical charge my body generated. Seeds of all sorts had become attached to me. Initially I shook myself in an effort to dislodge them. Then I haltingly stopped. The seeds refused to detach; the pollen also. My rational mind demanded a reason. I promptly shut down that line of inquiry and realized "rationality" is a system of logic that is too restrictive. My interpretations were led to wander—to free up in the anomaly, to be for once fully immersed in the atmosphere: the total ecological surround that is also in and through me, what I consist of and what has generated me.

The seeds were of many genuses: long tendrilled seeds, seeds short and thorny, seeds attached to silken threads. My body could feel their potentiality. I could feel my body respond as an incubator, a surrogate somehow making myself available as host and protector. Was I to travel with the seeds somewhere? Was the intention that I bury myself somewhere with the seeds still attached to me? The seeds hummed. The seeds emitted a frequency that I was able to hear—the hearing was a feeling that radiated throughout my body. I felt the presence of the seeds intensely on my person.

I felt the seeds worlding. Making space anew. I wanted reason but reason was already present, through the reaching of flowers, the plurality of being, and the breakdown of my unique "I"—at least the way in which one has been trained to believe in the structure of personhood; these seeds hold expansive knowledge of the world, having created the world already, and all of this is contained inside me, as it always had been.

What was the real fear I had? What was my body reacting to? What was my shaking a reaction *to*? Were these important questions to ask?

Seed 1: [insert movement diagram]

Seed 2: [insert movement diagram]

Seed 3: [insert movement diagram]

Had I been granted a divergent new role by the seeds? I felt like I had been elected to do something of which I wasn't sure—such is the demeanor of sentient life, new interactions and demands appearing on an ongoing basis. Questions abounding. Relations creating divergent pathways for experience. Between me and the seeds, our mutual opportunism united in a flurry of feelings.

Intense emotion prickled my entire body—an alternative body ideal, a being-together in complexity. This assemblage of seed, pollen, and person produced a plural "I." We were entangled in a rhythm. An arc of being. I wanted earnestly to be with them. They decided I should dedicate my life to their well-being. Said in another way: *we* as a plural matrix came to an unspoken decision to fruit together. The seeds buzzed and agitated my epidermal layer. *We will circulate and spread, we will grow together.* Fear dissipated and was replaced by elation. I rolled around in the dirt where the trees and underbrush had been growing and then had been felled. I rolled around to pick up more seeds, to make contact with the soil, the ground. Maybe more seeds would attach, would be attracted to this "I" that was becoming plural. Incompleteness begs coming together. A gathering has occurred. New possibilities make complacency obsolete.

[Insert: image of seeds and bodies rolling]

We—the seeds and myself and the seeds and myself and the rest of the world—hurtle through the air. Because everything is in everything. I must find myself in the seeds, and the seeds within me. Because we are in the air and this climate together, we must be as compassionate as we are intertwined. I must encourage the seeds and pollen to penetrate my being, only, I trampled the seeds just moments ago because seeds contain our freedom. I too must contain the liberation of us all—because the seed *is*; I will *be*.

[Insert: image of burning bushes]

It made total sense that the seeds saw my torso as a trunk. I now understand how I resembled a tree. I am a tree. Recently I have thought deeply of being rooted. I was actively looking for a place to anchor myself. No longer did I want to feel wayward and unsettled. My move to this new locale was mostly about finding a place to habituate. The town I entered had emptied out. Humans evidently found the town undesirable. Humans had vacated the region. As I cycled around, I found myself immersing myself. I found that the welcome committee was flora, fauna, and minerals. Covered with seeds and pollen, an ecosystem clung to my being.

A squirrel scurrying up an old moss-covered wall. Another squirrel digging in the tall, dry grass. I extend my arms out like rigid branches. I ground myself, trying to project my energy downward like roots that descend into the center of the earth, energy shooting out from the base of my forehead to create a line of connection with the sky, my arms mixing with the air, an attempt at stability, an attempt at interchange and osmosis, and at the moment I find my breath, an even inhale and exhale, I feel a thonk on my right arm. A squirrel has landed on my arm-branch, has mistaken me for a tree, and has decided to trust my foundation in this landscape. I turn my head to meet the squirrel's gaze, careful not to move my arm, to steady myself in the posture of a sessile being. Does he wonder why this tree has eyes? Or does he see the difference between trees and other-than-tree people at all?

The squirrel began eating the seeds in my hair. I could hear him, his low murmur echoed through my cranium as I adjusted my concentration. My focus was his voice. His chewing was active as his thinking was simultaneous. Images entered my thought-stream that were his. His projections, his observations, they coursed through my consciousness. I was looking down from a towering redwood.

I'm searching for seeds. The tree has not produced seeds. I, the squirrel, realize I must descend from the tree's crown, find a different tree, and continue my search for seeds elsewhere. My sense of being up in a tree, at its highest boughs, where my weight as a human would have caused me to lose balance was casual, normal. I feel no fear around scaling a tree and wandering far out onto the thinning branches.

The squirrel's hunger is my hunger as an impulse to climb and forage. While being the squirrel, I am a tree. I am a duality triplicating and then multiplying further in fractals of persons and ambient conditions. I am a morphing simultaneity, curiously. The flickering differences awaken me to place and space and time and being. I regurgitate and relive life.

I, as the squirrel, look back at the tree, who I still am also. But I am also the seeds in my hair, I am also my hair, I am also the space between entities, energies. My teeth grind together momentarily. I run over the dirt and stop briefly on my hind legs to scan the area around me. I am looking for seeds, for nuts. I remember a spot where one may be buried. I remember a spot I may have staked out to bury a nut in the future. What has happened already or, what has yet to occur? I clasp my paws together and I smell something burning or it has burned already and I am smelling an aftermath of an occurrence.

I erode in the wind and grow a tail as my torso becomes a trunk. My relationship to the world is reverential and sticky. A glue that sticks me to others is also what makes me whole. As a tree, fire becomes threatening. As a squirrel, a forest fire may threaten my kin. As a human, I understand fire is more than the sum of its parts. Fire, chemical reactions: combustion, conflagration. Making of materiality, dust. When fire is introduced, seeds are prompted to grow. Heat activates cells. I jump on my bike with the squirrel in my hair with my body covered in seeds with my consciousness swelling in floral and faunal becoming. Sweating, I pedal toward the smoke.

I'm on the bike riding toward the plumes of burnt matter. I'm losing leaves, furling off my branches due to the speed. I'm not used to movement in this manner. I'm grasping onto the human's shoulder with my claws, the hair in clumps shielding my face from the wind. I feel the squirrel's claws digging into my flesh but the pain is negligible. My bark is thick and solid and it has felt the feet of countless squirrels before. I am breathing. I am breathing. I, too, am breathing.

Breathing sucks the wind into the lungs, sucks oxygen into the ventricles. Breathing brings smoke, the human, myself, and the tree together, as atmosphere: we draw in smoke and smoke activates us in catastrophe. Catastrophe is engendering us to what was pronounced previously, to what was summoned—interior subjectivity, inside as around. Thickness—thick directions. Thick, myriad forms. Countless. Squirrels. Our hunger. Our reimagining as if moving like neon blurs in a video installation. Our host, the rider, pulls us toward genre to showcase to the public our myriad attitudes, our complicated expressions as it all becomes fused into personhood or prose or skyline breathline or smoke. Who lit the forest, the town? What was the consortium of wind, of bark, of seeds, of smoke drawing out as fuel for an ecological meltdown? We move toward the atmospheric changes as atmospheric change. We feel the metal from the deep earth where our roots channel, to those depths—the depths of the skies should not be overlooked.

I inhale again, deeply, following the breath, intermingled with the smoke and ashes and dust, following it down into my belly, the ashes from the fire out there feeding the fire in my belly, and I am the breath too, I am the smoke, and the skin of my body, like the leaves of the trees as permeable and open, mediating the climate of the world. I am tired. I want to sleep. We are weary.

The squirrel indicates, then gesticulates to me that the Brute caused the fire. The squirrel adamantly repeats "Brute." "The Brute." The Brute caused the fire. *Who is the Brute?* I ask, as an act of mental telepathy rather than as an actual sentence that formulates on my lips. I want to be brought into awareness of the Brute. *Who?* I ask, *is the Brute and where are they now?* The squirrel, without hesitation looks at me and says definitively, *You— you are the Brute.* Righteous indignation floods my nerve centers, surges through my veins. I ask pleadingly, plangently: *Me? You mean me?* The squirrel chuckles and looks distracted. He begins to focus on something else. He refuses to speak with me or engage further. He hunkers down, solemnly. *Ok*, he says to me, *I will interrogate myself.*

"I am the Brute," I say out loud to feel the designation—take it in. Feel the shape and form of the name I don't recognize. The "I" that is me has a second body—that of the Brute. The squirrel could see this fact clearly. I was slow to the claim. I am not an insular, insufficient creature—I am part of the gigantic throbbing whole. I am a co-creator of human disposition. The crimes of humanity are crimes I've committed. The crimes are crimes in my name. I burst into tears, seeds falling from my crown. I begin to sweat. I roll on the ground. I'm having a fit as I panic, and then feel a modicum of calm. The squirrel consoles me. My bark is wet. As I convulse I feel silly and also remorseful. I am overcome by the smoke. The squirrel bites on my fingernail. Then he bites on my ear lobe. He is trying to help me regain my equilibrium.

As breath, I move seamlessly in and out of bodies. Fill all the spaces between, create the entirety of the world with my very being. As smoke, I am carried with wind currents, stowaways of particles that once were also me, solid me, another form. As a tree, I am more patient. These things take time. All stories are at first about deterioration but only consider human scale. At cosmic scale there is always and ever the joining of all, the being, the making. I can wait it out, that is, we can persist and more will be made. Who said trees were passive? Even if human vision doesn't see us moving or acting, we have shaped a world in which it is possible for us to all coexist. There is coexistence or nothing. And nothing is impossible. Nothingness. I sob into the ground and my tears soak the soil and my toes wriggle toward the moisture. I scurry down the trunk and remember where I buried a peanut earlier in the day, pushing the wet soil aside with my paws.

The bike skidded. I fell off the bike. I must have hit pay dirt. Blood dripped down my cheeks onto my lips. I felt dazed. A lump formed on my forehead. I looked around for my belongings but there were none. Just a bike that was now broken, so I sat beside it. Re-piecing events did not yield a more conclusive picture. Suddenly I didn't know where I was. Had the head injury I just suffered given me momentary amnesia? I wasn't sure of anything. Had I been struck? There was a squirrel near me and I recognized him as a familiar. Our friendliness was apparent. Intuitively I trusted him. He licked my wounds. I felt strange and grateful. I stroked his fur. We settled into a solemn quietude.

The glistening of slick concrete. Has it rained recently? The lingering petrichor affirms this and the lingering question, too: how to recenter what has already always been at the center, or, how to rebalance toward a system without any center at all, without categories or binaries or even frontiers?

Excuse me, what is the status of the fire?
Excuse me, where do you come from?

Pardon this query but, why are we running away?
Hello, yes. Hello. Have you always been here?
But, I didn't see you there.
But, I didn't know.
But, wait a moment.

Scurry scurry hurry hurry.
Oh mama, llama drama.

•

[Insert image of tree branch reaching earthward]

As the landscape, I breathe.

I came down with a fever: heavy panting, sweating. I was on fire. The squirrel didn't abandon me. As my body raged, my mind raged, the landscape raged. Passion, emotion, sexual energy came forward like a devil of consequence, like an angel of consideration, like smoke smoldering and fire chewing to the core of presence. Whatever was burning was burning to the core—being incinerated back to primal ash. Fire has a hunger like no other. I felt like a devil about to burst. Breathing was difficult but then, gradually, I caught my wind. I didn't know where I was, but I was curious and mystified by the fire. I couldn't just ignore it. I placed the squirrel back in my bushy head of hair and began walking in the direction of the flames. My mother's face burned as a hologram in front of me. My father's face. Then my sister's and brother's—their countenances like glowing embers, hallucinations, spirits. I saw a mountain of flame and an ocean engulfed by fire. I witnessed squirrels rushing from their dreys into the woods, all aflame. What I experienced was a fever dream as I headed toward an actual fire. In reality the surroundings were on fire. The sound was deafening, popping; structures were imploding, bursting. The squirrel stayed close to my scalp. I saw a river, and I paused to splash water on us, on my arms that looked scaly and dry like bark and on my face that burned like the sun.

[Insert image: close-up of a squirrel's face]

I caught my breath in the wind. Up in her hair I was shaken about and then splashed by water, my eyes burned as we drew near the inferno. I had asked to be doused by water from the river because exposing fur to flames is usually a death sentence. Angels and isotopes: that is the equation I could overhear in her brain. I felt comfortable in the tree and her boughs still had their leaves. She was notably autonomous while simultaneously varied, a kaleidoscope of the surround—a walking, breathing interchangeable entity with ample spirit—an energy that realized her body among bodies as a symbiotic whole. I began to mimic her as I knew she was mimicking me. The human species crossed a threshold. How, we weren't sure. The human grew into everything—this tendency was translated everywhere—everybody not human had to, by necessity of survival, grow out of sameness into variegated brilliance.

The human tendency was monocultural, for many reasons. But no modality was complete or dominant, there were limits. The cells of difference within the monoculture rebelled. I united with the tree and we metabolized reality. We designed paradigms and practiced a collaboration for the moment.

How to arrive at the fire—understand the fire—in ourselves as a reflection of the totality, the totality of cosmic and terrestrial wholeness? The terms spread as the implications spread: to the far reaches, away from cities. The trees were imported by the city because the native trees had been razed. Outsider trees had to be introduced. Some trees escaped human control—there was possibility for noncompliance—proving that apex predators had their built-in limitations, blind spots, ignorance, and lazy hearing. Diversity lies in cells. DNA doesn't forget arrays.

The introduced trees were of Asian origin, European origin, African origin. The globalization of flora and fauna had been a fact for a hundred years, a thousand years, more. The trees had no familiarity of the space and place they now inhabited. Their removal created conditions of loneliness and forlornness. They were nonconsensual immigrants. Yet there was new community, new spaciousness.

Trees are an interface and trees are a module of an urban planning strategy. In this view, their personhood is ignored. The trees reject the grid. The grid is nonsense. Root systems strive to break through concrete. Seedlings and pollen and seeds, with all their power of sexual activity and floatation devices, work against the grid. The wind and the seeds work in collaboration to promote life.

Humans don't prefer to eat most seeds produced by trees and other flora, so for the most part seeds have been safe from human exploitation. We told stories amongst ourselves about the potency of seeds. Seeds are so terrific because seeds understand and maximize solar power and like little spaceships, seeds cruise here and there and stake out places quite nonchalantly, land, wait for moisture, and sprout. The sun is the mighty energy source that nurses the seed, furious with explosions lifting off its surface. Burning away millions of miles from Earth, seemingly antithetical yet a sustaining force, the sun is an ally—a benevolent power and, equally, a threat.

There are recurring patterns of master plot where nurturer overcomes destroyer, but you can't nail down either pole. The nurturer can have a bad mood and blast excess vitriol to earth, radiating sentient life too forcefully. Still, the sun has a predictable rhythm that is dependable—day and night are accountable to the sun.

In this reverie I was hallucinating a pathway through contradictory paradigms. I was riding in the crown of a tree—the tree's mobility set me in motion along with its extending branches and leaves.

The seeds were sustaining, nourishing, delicious. I didn't eat too many. I realized reforesting the ecosystem was crucial. Every seed contains a vision of a forested multispecies community, but "species" is an obscene way to think of life. As if it were possible to cordon off characteristics; as if it could be possible or conceivable, or even desirable. I ate the seeds, internalizing seedness, forestness.

My night soil will become a garden, my tongue tangled in forests in fecundity and friendship. The psychic links become physical links. I consider myself a friend of the trees and I dream of our togetherness under the sun as the sun rages on, far away, like a furious genius. The sun is relentless, going 24-7 without losing a stroke of fury. Burning all day and night—an encircling inferno, circulating power in the form of radiation. There is no redundancy in necessity. The seeds in my stomach ache internally. Flora joins flora, as fauna converts to flora, resurging again as fauna. The sun creates the necessity of eyes. Illumination craves sight. Crisis mobilizes crisis energy—we ride it out. It is a stimulus. The tree is undulating. Now the tree is moving as if trotting; for a moment I imagine I'm riding horseback.

Fire draws its fuel in a strange attractive pull. The fire is a seduction, calling the tree. Why do I ride along? Is it more ethical to beg the tree to stop here? Give up the pursuit of fire? I'm not into pulling apart philosophical tautologies. The trajectory we are on is being moved along by many simultaneous forces.

[Insert image: left eyeball of a bird of the deep rainforest]

The sun introduces us to each other.

As the sun, I look down over a land of words. As the sun, landscapes are infinite archives and blasts of fire within my belly radiate out from my center like an explosion of bats at twilight, like the words shaking loose hundreds of seeds from flexible branches, like a can of soda shaken too hard from a vigorous bike ride. I breathe too, as sun, I am still one of many, one of all. There is no "the" sun, I simply *am*, pulsate, bellow, breathe. Energy cycling in and out and the serpent activated by the fire of my belly. It is focus that will allow me to transfer energy outward. Porous light. Permeable gratitude. Archived explosion. Which seed does not incinerate, but flourish, inside a fire? Whose skin does not burn away when exposed to infinite radiation? Can the energy produced from a cry of pain be metabolized into light?

"Whose land?"
"My land."
"Who's speaking?"
"Me."
"What is a 'me'?"
"A self."
"I only see you."
"Exactly."
"Insufficient data."
"I'm me."
"False statement."
"I'm true."
"You *are*. But you are not *yourself*."
"But I am compostable?"
"You have already been composted, are already integrated."

I find it more and more difficult to keep it all contained, to keep myself contained in this body. What is excess if there is no containment? What is contamination if there are no barriers? What is home if there are no walls? What is permanence if you were never born? What is excess if we resist the desire to contain?

[*Missing stage directions:*
Person is confused. Not sure which bin they should go into:
LANDFILL / RECYCLING / COMPOST]

"Hello, how are you?"
"I'm on fire."

[Insert image: infinite compost heap]

The tree intensifies greenness; green is the fur of the earth.

The sun was a blazing glare, gassy and opulent. Squirrels scurried everywhere. Sight was obscured; the smoke hid the line of vision. The smoke cleansed. Dust settled on the surface of the soil. The sky vanished. A sense of self was co-opted by worldliness. Fixating on greenness felt comfortable—on blueness, on brownness. Birds in the distance cried "mee mee, me me meee." The tree was moaning. Their vocables were low-pitched murmurs that caused the hair on my arms to sway with static electricity.

Squirrel speaking presently: "My hair is standing on end!"

The individuals who had collectively razed the expanse were far gone inside goneness, to a remote location. Like a special club: exclusive. People are the government, people are society. People are communal.

Brown and green and blue were all over. What drew us to the fire: red, bold, orange, bold. There was a war on the soil and a war on the rocks, even though soil and rock were weapons. How one conceptualizes is how one cares.

Or? As a small marmot I prefer to be open about the traps of language and how we assume our bodies are impenetrable. My pupils flicker within meanings. I probe the universe of meanings by listening to rocks and soil.

I don't know how to be emotionally invested. My paw trembles. The tree limps. I sang yesterday about the leaves. My fruiting body fields all of their questions. The response is annexed. The ground shakes or will shake again. The soil is a membrane. I collect particles. We occupy the same space. We *are* the space. And yet —

There is a fear that if I allow myself to spill out of this membrane that my self will disintegrate, that is, the ethereal self inside me I'm trying to protect, as if my soul can't be let out, can't be contaminated. And if I fell out, fell apart, I would just rejoin the soil, the soil I always was and always will be, while the worms tirelessly labor below our feet and without our gratitude. We push them to work faster. There is an urgency to our desire, our desire to be individual becomes an impulse for dominion over others, that individuality slides so quickly into hierarchy, and if I leave the dirt where I found it, what will grow there?

I carry fear as if it were an unborn person in my womb. A sense of foreboding grows and I nurture it in my body by feeding it my anxieties. Amplifying volition, stoking the flames of fear, I often triumph in creating the bold fright monster, greedy of overloaded emotional content. This doppelganger of distress likes to pose as me. She wears the clothing I wear. She banishes me to a dull corner while, melodramatically, she gesticulates.

The squirrel has helped me innumerably to see and understand that I have been giving sanctuary to an energy that needs space to roam, not cling to me. Now I've opened the portals and fear, the great narcissist slips out looking for attention elsewhere.

A quotient of fear keeps alertness heightened. Fear connects to fear, and through fear I connect to and find my agency. Sensing fear in others offers intimacy between parties. Let's promise not to kill each other. How long should a promise last?

I would hope our skills and competency be respected and prove to be generative for others, to share in a newfound movement of interspecies care work.

Your suffering is my suffering, not as possessive property but rather as a mutual, psychic, somatic atmosphere.

All plants feel all plants' pain.

A plant will seek an animal to assuage their pain. An animal will seek out a plant to ease her pain. When we are bitten into, gently, with great care, we re-body ourselves: we are re-embodied. This sharing of our bodies is the method that allows us to go home. I recognize you in my body as my body, as you do, also. Misrecognition is a danger of great magnitude. Thus, we need to pet each other and taste each other continually to remain focused on our mutuality.

The inner child is also a mountainous realization. From volcanic origins of fear, upward to a pinnacle out of the mouth of hell toward sheer sky. She grows mighty and snow-covered. She provides the space for mountains and valleys. From rumbling tentativeness comes open land unrolling. The taste of the mountain is salty and mineral rich.

As we approached the raging fires my fear blossomed into a freedom beyond ownership. I no longer "owned" my emotions nor my body nor my imagination. All was contiguous, intertwined. The fire gave me courage and strength—clarity. The fire excited anger. The fire brought the combustion of gasses and metal to the fore. I located the water in my cells and asked the water to support me in the face of fire.

We are an immigrant diaspora of flora and fauna heading as if to a family reunion. What we find is fire. Human history claims man began to manage fire, thus transforming from ape to human.

We are using fire to transform out of the human into earthlings without species taxonomy. We don't allow bigotry of the squirrel, bigotry of the rat, bigotry of the goat, the snake, the sparrow. Our sublime eyes are beaches of gathering and our limbs are stories like canoes traveling to where we came from, traveling between when and when.

Trees define us; the trees open up silence as an evanescent beckoning. The trees define the sun's edicts. The laws are of the sun and moon and earth as a triangle of mineral origin that is inclusive of the entire cosmos. A detailed Doppler image doesn't reveal the sun's charisma with floral and faunal persons. Minerals too are drawn in by the sun. A sunspot of the surface of the sun has a mighty magnetic field, ranging in strength up to 10,000 times that of the Earth's magnetic field.

My life's goal is to ask: *Do you know where you are?* as an urgent question of transformation. Forgetting as a way of unmaking a terrible system and awaken lucky togetherness that won't lock any moment in any place.

The military apparatus demands the mugshot, the selfie, recognizable statistics. However, we change so much we can't be pinned down—our portraits morph. We cultivate the power of slippage. We slide away from discriminatory profiling. If you think you "know" by what you think "it" looks like, this is a devastating situation that requires fire.

Thus, the data center exploded. The stereotypes were too multiple. The data center was working on overload to store the stereotypes. We were most likely dead—thus alive. We see everyone dying, yet living in death. We awaken in our deaths as a dark ultraviolet light. Shadow and light mediate powerful flow. The finite has already occurred. We are respooling the future.

I hold my paw out in front of me, palm upwards, absorbing sunlight, dust motes floating down and around, and I turn my paw over, relaxing, stretching, pushing that newly received solar energy down into the ground. As I push energy down, mediated through my own flesh, my breath intermingles with the sun's fiery exhalations, and in turn I draw upward the earthy energy and warmth of the mulching soil. The center of this particular planetary body, the entire underworld, is channeled through one squirrel's beckoning, a beckoning that simply occurs through the act of an extended paw. I hold out my paw as a gesture of encounter—an extended appendage creates a point of future intimacy. I multiply into numerous beings.

Here—my paw—energy radiating in all directions—is the gathering place for the breaths of thousands, no, millions of squirrels, intermeshed with the humans, the trees, the fire, the world, all the worlds.

One palm to another. One gaze to another. I see you. I see you. I see you.

Here are the accretionary generations of communities accumulating through the sun's expansion and the earth's mulching of our dead bodies, channeled into our current vibrant beings. We are surging. I hold my paw over my hind leg, slowly move my other paw over my other hind leg, my lower body, my belly. The moving and pulsing of energy feels like waves that gently guide my paw slowly up my body until it reaches my heart. Something delays my paw right before it connects with the organ in my chest. There is a blockage. What is required is a generative removal of the abscess; it is hot, burns my paw and I can't move any further. *Ow*, I yelp. I bring in my other paw to aid in this illumination. I twine my paws around each other, attempt to wrangle and unbind the invisible yet utterly felt wound from my chest. Now my breathing is fraught and strained, the sensation burning its way into my heart and growing like a tumor or inflammation. I twine my paws with intense focus, with intense light and breath as received from the sun and earth and generous plant beings around me. The tree has now joined in. The tree twines her hands, wrist over wrist, and then, as if precisely choreographed or mentally telepathized we both begin to pull the invisible threads of misplaced fury and grief, grief that has no appropriate outlet and has been contained forcefully within my chest, as I had hardened myself from the outside world in an unconscious effort to cope and survive. The threads slowly unbind, we pull them out, and once exiting my body and exposed to the atmosphere, they immediately become part of the atmosphere and dissipate naturally and effortlessly. The treads are pulled out like words, words of an excessive or endless sentence, because the author can't place a period after the string of words without the consent of the squirrel gesticulating and enacting its own performance in the sanctimonious system, or as I, human, begin sobbing, I, the squirrel, feel lighter and airier and I realize my increased vitality and mobility, this act of self-care becomes a small act of rebalancing the entire cosmos, or, as the stars watch each other, one of the bright solar bodies exists as a corporeal statement and encourages me to continue without the pain of solastalgia, because the erosion of our identities is not the erosion of our vitality, because our fusion of self is not a cause to grieve, and because I can stand for prolonged periods of time on my two hind legs, the human sees me as familiar and endearing; I allow the human to feed me seasoned rice, the language of her expression entering my body; my tail quivers. I am not hungry, but I eat anyway. I am not tired. The sun is bright, and I close my eyes, taking respite from brilliance.

CONFERENCE

A kindly person approached me in the breakfast nook. The person was gray-haired and gentle. He stood quietly in front of me as breakfast-goers milled about the offerings of cereal and fruit on display in the little motel restaurant. He asked me how to navigate to the Hart building on campus. Initially I couldn't locate it on the map. Then I noticed it was in the Quad. Within the Quad lived the softest, greenest feather tree, a luminous bald cypress that undulates in the wind. We'd passed them many times, sought them out, because the tree exuded such generosity, dignity, and grace. The tree seemed to beckon us. I wondered if the man would encounter the tree on his way to the Hart building. I drew a map on a fluorescent green Post-it note I grabbed from the motel office and gave it to him. The directions were: *left, left, right, directly across the street from the garden with the mimosa and the gurgling fountain, you will have reached your destination*. The man accepted the map with the scribbles and headed off. I watched his body foreshorten in the distance, his gray braids swaying side to side as his form diminished within the ecological whole. He wore a baseball cap with an insignia of feathers. As he turned the corner, all I could see was the top of his hat.

The university was originally an agricultural school; plants and trees grew in profusion throughout the spacious campus that once contained a farm. There were pathways that entered into thick densities of plant populations; diverse cohabitational communities of flora living in various complex configurations designed by humans. We walked along the pathways at different times of the day, maneuvering our way to various buildings where panels with an environmental focus were being held.

Briefly separated from my colleague, I found myself again, under the tutelage of the cypress tree, grateful for the tree's directional knowledge that radiated from their branches, trunk and roots connecting sun and sky with earth. I drifted to a cluster of redwood trees thickly needled where countless spiders were living within the boughs—a cosmic matrix of threads. The diamond fluff suspended between the needles was home to numerous spiders who called the redwoods their home. What a superb place to live one's destiny within the sanctity of a breathing stand of trees! Four trees showed solidarity with one another; they were clearly a family unit, growing together throughout their lives. The mundane intimacy of their togetherness is a story about sugar, sunlight, water, sky, minerals—and spiders.

A single feather from a peregrine falcon drifted toward me from the sky. It dangled in the air, suspended on the currents. I caught it before it landed on the surface of the earth. I walked among the trees. Someone had placed a bowl of food for the stray cats on campus. One gray cat came to dine. The feeling was normal and wondrous.

My colleague and I met for a panel on "The Madness of Nuclear Fallout." Insanity is posited as a form of resistance to the ubiquity of nuclear weaponry. Even when weapons are not deployed, they cause environmental damage because they are nearly impossible to store in a nonthreatening way long-term. The toxic aftermath of poisoned environments and bodies was the focus of the discussion at hand. Once humans entered the nuclear age, it seems there was no turning back. To detangle from the exigencies of nuclear threat was an epic challenge, a lagging conundrum.

Other panels focused on wide-ranging topics that intersected culture and nature, human and other-than-human. One discussion concerned night soil in regard to nation-building, another, the neglected lives of micro-matter as pertaining to river amoeba and outbreaks of contagion. We listened in on presentations about green imperialism that begins after death, when bodies break down and matter reconfigures. Our notetaking scratched the epidermis of tree matter or deep-earth materials while we sat in chairs made of metal and plastic in rooms glowing with a mix of artificial and natural light. Between panels we circumnavigated the spread-out campus, with concrete pathways managing our every step. The friction of our steps sparked a low-level energy field. Several times a day we passed a grand white sage that communicated messages quite frankly. We found the sage to have a spicy personality. The sage did not mince emotions. ("Frankly, my dear, I don't give a damn!") My colleague photographed me next to this incredible person with their glowing white-gray spray of limbs spanning out toward the sky. I photographed her imbricated with gigantic artichoke flowers. The praxis of enriched landscapes, the georgics of dwelling in what we do. Sometime after sundown we retreated to the little motel, collapsing in our beds, continuing on with our discussions...

The following day my colleague left hours before I had to head to the airport. I imagined her flying with strangers in a huge, metal, bird-like contraption through the sky. The atmosphere was different without her presence, yet a second self, an afterglow, lingered and traipsed with me.

The man who asked for directions to the Hart building the morning before in the breakfast nook was standing in front of the little motel where my colleague and I had stayed. He had also stayed there with his partner in that little motel for the duration of the conference. Obviously, that was why he too was in the breakfast nook the day before. He and his partner were waiting for their ride. I approached him and asked him how he had experienced the conference. He said the conference had surpassed his expectations. He had come to discuss efforts to keep his language alive and the conference had given him renewed hope, and a sense of momentum. I gave him the feather from the peregrine falcon and wished him a safe journey.

The soft intimacy of the day was warming. The air molecules were expanding. Consciousness is combustible, apt to catch aflame.

The symmetries of the world attune.

We are not in an insane asylum, and everyone is not insane. People might have an imbalance of fire and water or air and earth. As the planet is reengineered to resemble restrictive institutional space, the imbalances become acute.

Fire incites heavy metals which cause downward spirals. Downward spirals resemble black holes of emptiness and sorrow. Heavy metals are agents from deep earth and intergalactic nighttimes that are able to recuperate the power of explosiveness and send sentience into powerful kernels of nothingness where energy pools, amalgamates, waits. When heavy metals magnetize spirit there is a tendency to spiral downward, so deeply inward as to lose identity, as to injure the soul. Heavy metals are responsible for brain death. Heavy metals understand endlessness and silence and are able to produce silence with radioactive certainty.

The certainty of the twine that unravels and interlocks, ends and begins, begins and ends, wrapping like tendrils around my body. Have I dozed off? Am I in a trance of some sort? The twine grows around my body, my limbs, the table, the garden, the woods, the silence; a small heap of tiny ripples form undulating waves of rot and black dust and I scrape at them with fingernails but I am only scratching my own skin—loosening gray, ashy bits of dry skin, the cymbals echoing in the distance like the beginning of a Hollywood movie and I am growing all around myself—I am reaching out like tendrils, stretching into myself and from opposite ends and from behind my ears and under my tail, and the scraping of my fingernails which grow outward, coursing heaps of fingernails that smell like rot, and the strongest memory is of the dog snoring, his dark nose slightly twitching, the calm breath that escapes between sighs, one paw twitching forward, the other paw tucked beneath his beard, his sighs blowing air and rustling the beard hairs, and as I watch, here are the tendrils suffocating, and I clench my fists, my body, I clench everything, but like quicksand it squeezes me more and more tightly and I can't breathe, and the struggle to breathe quickens the squeezing and I smell the dead, rotting corpse of my future self but I am still here / I AM STILL HERE / and I am still trying to breathe, still trying to breathe, still fighting, fighting, fighting, resisting, resisting, resisting, but what is it that I am resisting in this winding up of twine, growing around the legs and tail from opposite ends, swallowing me up in my own proprioceptive tank of yielding to rotting apples—throw the rotten ones out, throw the ones with holes out, throw them all out, heaps of garbage growing and the stench of it, the stench of rotting garbage that reaches like tendrils into my nostrils and back behind my ears, the ashy black dust of rot, the blacks of my eyes turning back into my head—I am stretching myself away from that smell but my fingernails continue growing toward the heaps, reaching to scratch my own back that is now in front of me / I AM STILL HERE / the table is shaking because my legs are shaking because the tendrils are shaking me, my body still clenched, still holding on to the act of filling my holes with the external validation of the heaps of rotting apple cores, still holding on to keeping my guard up, so bravely dismissing any chance for vulnerability, so bravely being a coward in the garbage pile, so bravely ready to say goodbye before it is time to say goodbye, and as a pinprick of light makes its way through the clouds—light-touched dust motes scatter and dance in front of my eyes—I loosen my body just because and I loosen my body because the other way is no way to live and I loosen my body because the clenched, white-knuckled self is no way to live, is not a posture that is conducive to life, that sustains life, so I open my arms out to embrace the light, to embrace the climate of cyclical breath and the light allows air and the air allows light and the body allows vulnerability and the vulnerability allows love and the open arms allow intimacy and the intimacy allows seeing and the seeing allows for more seeing, a growth that doesn't invade or colonize but is becoming, not from opposite ends, because opposites don't exist, but from the center outward, and from within. All of it, from within. I wander around the woods at night and scratch the wooden table with my fingernails. The splinters remind me of the damage I've done. I remind myself that I deserve to tell my story too.

Twine represents the life force as it unspools into destiny's inscrutable dense and oftentimes opaque waters. Feeling tangled and also, feeling restrained by the twine, I look to other forms of entanglement and other forms of restraint that bind me to reality. It is a bit odd to me that I don't remember the context of a trauma that continues to wrap me in its embrace. When hit with the lingering symptoms of distress, breathing becomes frantic and I have to pause and follow a breath back into the body and out again, as the breath makes a pathway through the earth's atmosphere returning to my lungs. I really like the description of the rotting apples—an orchard cluttered with the debris of spongy apples decomposing sourly and sweetly. There's the image also of a trough of rancid apples, the juice fermented, the foam on the top layer swaying slightly as maggots and fruit flies giddily squirm and buzz over and within the vat. No evidence but the memory persists. I remember the argument, an internal dialogue as to why this incident caused me grief. I have had to come to explain and defend this image to myself, even with my faulty memory of the incident. Because I can't fully remember, I've had to improvise the details, contribute to what the site of my trauma could have held. I occasionally rehearse this recollection as a performance of obstinacy. Without the remnants of the faded memory, trauma would persist, divorced of its dimensional texture.

Piecing together fabricated strands of information troubles me less than a stand-alone traumatic fact. One realization becomes clear: I harmonize with trauma—the events of the past that haunt me and trauma in all of its modes. Trouble imposed externally becomes lived, internal reality. Neither the trauma experienced as one's bodily reality or outside its membrane are static. Trauma is a storyline that takes me in and out of myself, a body with a skin barrier bordering upon the broader world. At times I can't wrap my head around the specter of drama, and I assume the role of instigator, boiling out thicker details that evade the mushy archive of recollection. Psychically repeating the trauma is deviant activity. Each iteration slightly skews the data.

The twine wraps around my neck in a chokehold. The twine snakes between my crotch and legs and suspends me in a sexualized pose. When I'm suspended above the ground, with the twine connected to the ceiling, I dangle as if drifting through the sky. The floor falls away and my body is lithe, airborne, seedlike. The twine stakes the flowers and protects from the impact of the wind, and as a self-representation, I identify as floral. Floral in a feminist sense, as ecologically integral, and also floral as a resonant frequency, identifying with the tonality of floral sonic pitch. Twine is, of course, plant based. Plant fiber is a resilient material. My elective affinity is where newly possible forms of friendship are kindled.

The philosopher (who identifies as such, yet also has a contentious relationship with the term "philosopher") wrote a statement that relates to the problem of naming, as naming is how one is known forever after the name-giving event—by the description it carries. They wrote: "I think, from the fact that we are affected by the ways we are addressed, and these modes of address start early and against our will, they are there, as it were, from the start. Sometimes those modes of address embrace and animate, but they can inaugurate a chain of injury as well. So, from the start, we are affected, even if 'being ignored' or 'being called by injurious names' are the modes of address that affect us, install themselves in us, move or stop us in various ways." Extending what the philosopher expresses, beyond understandings of gender and race, to all forms of categorization, including the catch-all hegemonic category of "human" that tends to efface floral and faunal beingness, is the only way to unwind power dynamics as they exist. The assignment "human" grants undue authority and power over all other co-participant members of the earthly community.

You don't see it because you persist in the habits of judgement. I clamor to deviate; express how I am animated by other-than-human collaborators. The twine binds me to my roots. *We should talk.* The apples allude to an original trauma. The infancy of floral disparagement, that epoch is still with us.

Walking back along a sidewalk heading to my place of residence, there are paw prints patterned with blood on the concrete. I follow the pained steps of the dog, the bloodied steps continuing for several blocks. There in front of a telephone pole is a small dog, curled in a ball. It is clear the dog is dead. I vow to bring the dog to the forest to bury them there, under the pine trees, under the dim light of the forest canopy. The dog will become the forest. Bones trunks leaves fur foliage heart mineral tears roots.

I gather the dog up into my arms and walk to the forest's edge. I gather cedar leaves and soft stones for the ceremony. I gather coriander seeds and autumn mushrooms and lavender blossoms and holy sage. I gather plantain weeds and dried tea leaves and acorns and shards of beautiful, colored glass. I gather myself, all the parts of myself that are scattered throughout the forest and the city and the burning flames and all the parts of myself that are in the ashes of burned acres of land and all the parts of myself that are stuck in yesterday and the day before and in the anxiety of tomorrow and what is yet to come and I gather and I breathe, and I gather all of the breath and the strength of the earth below my feet and the fire from the earth's core and I join with the climate of the world, living and breathing and dying. The breath joins us in birth after rebirth, death after new death. Before the ritual I journey onto the sacred land, and before the entrance to the underworld I see the dog sleeping. His breath is calm and even and he seems content in his sleep, his paws twitching with the joy of dog-dream-sleep, and I sit down beside him on the sand. Feeling the pressure of my butt hitting the sand next to his head, he wakes for just a moment, looks up at me with a sleepy look, stretches out his mouth into a yawn, and returns to his own sleep-journey. Here is the dog, resting, dreaming, existing in the sacred space of our co-curated imaginal realm. Here, he is taken care of and will take care of me and here the balance remains intact. I return to the ordinary reality of the burning world (as I kneel here next to the singed forest, there are thousands of acres burning in the Amazon, the earth's lungs decimated and burning—how do humans so easily destroy so much life in a matter of moments, how do we so easily erase that which sustains us and keep moving forward, how do we? —) and I close my eyes in an attempt to return to the seat of my own sustenance. This dog becomes more than just one dead dog, but all of the dead dogs, all of the dead animals in the forest and in the Amazon, all of the needless deaths, the breakage of cycles and balance and resonance, all of it, here, already, always. So many are dead and yet I breathe.

Once, while sharing a dream with a teacher, she said to me, "What if every aspect of the dream was an aspect of you? Not just you, as *you*, in the dream, but that the sea anemone, the ocean, the bird, the dog, the sunset, your mother? Those are also all aspects of you." In this moment, I see the dead dog as an aspect of me, of the world, of everything. In the dog's body I see all of me and everything of me that ever was, is, and will be, in that soft, matted, bloodied fur, the closed eyes, the scabs on the paws, and because it is me that has also died here, I weep for all of us. I give my tears to the ground, and I give my tears to the dog, and I pray. I am not religious, and I never learned how to pray, but it seems appropriate right now to bring my own paws together in a solemn connection with all dead things and to pray for restoration, for attunement, for breath over and over again. It's as if I am learning how to want again. It's as if I'm learning how to breathe again. It's as if this, here, this moment, is the most important moment to have ever existed. That is, in the present it is the only moment, it is everything, and this burial is the most important ceremony.

I passed out on the forest floor and when I awoke it was night and the ritual I had conducted for the deceased dog I had found on the concrete sidewalk had synthesized with the night air. A few shards of colored glass shimmered within the night atmosphere, otherwise I couldn't see much beyond the trees at earth level. The sky was present and visibly a paler shade of purple-black. Around me the dark soil and huge metamorphic boulders balanced atop the soil exuded a state of equilibrium. Warm breath from my mouth created micro-clouds. A micro-climate of intensity surrounded me. I had matches on me but I didn't dare light a fire for fear that the tinder around me would ignite. Climbing atop a rock, I sat there gazing into the black of night that shrouded the familiar world. My posture eased. I was surprised how calm I felt, alone in the forest without shelter. The dog seemed to be transmitting warmth from beneath the surface of the forest floor. The infrastructure of the spell extended to the forest around me. Critical attention—that feeling of always being vigilant, had given way to total suspension.

Like a spider I hung on gossamer threads between worlds awash in molecules of energy—a web of hospitality. The nature of my thinking was different. Objectless? Mourning for the dog had relocated the gravity. An epistemic gateway had shaken loose. Breathing out here on a rock was a feeling of completion. The air was soft and powerful and in alternate breaths, acrid and filled with burning. A high-pitched squeal equalized a low tonal rumble. The trees trilled like glasses of water rubbed around their rims to emit a resonant frequency. When energy courses through material it vibrates. The energy of the ritual was reverberating. The fires were reverberating. Every breathing body was reverberating. The reuptake was happening. The roots of the trees sensed the dog's body and were searching for him underground. The roots would reabsorb the dog, eventually giving the dog a home in the canopy.

There were no shadows, only the near total absence of light at ground level, under a waxing gibbous moon. The stars crowded the thick expanse with punctures of motion millions of years in age. The dog glowed as a revenant in my mind's eye as I watched the shimmering glass come to life. The dog had re-particularized as a second self, a companion spirit. We would walk the earth together until my body too would become a corpse. When I came to again, the sky was a dreamy pale-peach ocean and rain dampened my forehead. The horoscope had been prescriptive: *it's a day to let your mind fall apart like petals falling from a dying flower.* I took this literally and it became literal. As morning unraveled, I would move from the funeral and the forest toward the burning and the city. I would retrace the pathway that had led me here.

The information gleaned from this forest communicates the distress of the Amazon, a complex ecosystem thousands of miles away. The evisceration of a tapir, jaguar, rhino beetle, tree cutter ant resounds through biospheric membranes. Trauma presents itself as unimaginable fallout. Convection cycles transport air currents around the globe. Particulate matter is suspended in the clouds and rains down elsewhere. The sounds of the inferno also travel in voices of animals and plants turning into cinders. Breathing becomes compromised. Oxygen is reduced. The trees in this forest attempt to compensate for the loss of atmosphere.

Extractionists with necropolitical alliances are excited by the possibility of capitalizing on the loss of the forest and view its destruction as valuation. But when forests are felled, the social fabric is felled. Converting living, breathing entities into commodities is a form of asphyxiation on multiple levels.

I stammer out sounds, a low buzz emanating from my mouth. Deterioration of mind like a mouse skirting across the floor in the periphery of my vision. I turn to look, and only the shadow of a shadow presents. I am that shadow self. *Is this how we overcome death?* I wonder. Do we follow the ashes re-particularizing and somehow find ourselves on the other side? Do we allow ourselves to breathe more slowly—the reduction of air affects us all—and is catastrophe the only way to slow us all down, to slow down the entire global-capitalist machine that drives us, pushes us, faster, faster, faster still, and is it only the inability to breathe that steadies us to the heartbeat of the earth, dying, forlorn, but in sync? Is this how we reset our own rhythm to match that of the planet—people woven of limits, people woven of hallucinations, people woven of patterns of lashing out, incensed, increased, inbred, veneration of lack and denial? Aren't we all of humble births, and yet why the constant dispatching of troops to every border?

Why must everything be contained?

Rhythm is a syncopation of tempo, is a living inside death, and when I breathe, I sink deeper into the earth and people woven like shrouds, people woven like hungry ghosts, people woven of smoke and air and thirst and bursting, bursting, bursting. Such excitement, such glory, such delusion. Still, caressing time is lovely. I can barely walk but there is a home I feel I must return to. I'm not sure whose home, but I'm sure I will know when I arrive. I track which direction I should go, and I allow one foot to land in front of the other foot, and this pattern will somehow propel me toward some destination. I'm trying not to be so linear, not to be so point-A-to-point-B, but it seems that this is the only way humans can travel anywhere, and moving so consistently brings about a desire to manifest frameworks on top of the movement, that is, the urge to create signposts, the urge to go faster, the urge to impose limits to dampen the urge to go faster, the urge to break the rules set in place to dampen the urge to go faster, the urge to have an urge, people woven of light, people woven of speed, people woven of sound and singing and moving constantly, constantly, constantly. When I stop I will be dead, or so I've been made to believe.

Something whirring in the air. Helicopter blades? A UFO? I can feel the whooshing air and hear a kind of heavy roaring that reverberates throughout my body, but I lift my head to scan the sky and see nothing. People woven of surveillance, people woven of following orders, people woven of paranoia. The latest development is an announcement for the latest development. This is the news cycle. An update of an update of an update. But the real news is that there is no news, only the deterioration of the mind again, and as my nose starts to bleed, I only move faster, as if to outpace the blood circulating through me.

Delirium overcomes the breathing corpus. We were conditioned to expect that the circle of our isolation is irrevocable. The sun that breaks open our confusion abridges our mystification; either the sun or the tail of the cat will undo the vicious circles that beat out rhythms. Otherwise, persons are left with few viable options in the face of the regulations driving cultural mandates dictated by commerce, wielded by power. There is a sense of anticipation—that something will descend from elsewhere, from the troposphere, open a portal, complete a cycle, guarantee an outcome. I cling to my friend and my friend clings to me, as I realize that my friend is shadow and I am a ghost, often unavailable or discrete. My friend can't be located as to ever be "present." Again, the riddle of contemporary life where persons have the option to avail anything with a click of a keystroke and yet, the material doesn't materialize. Products of industry appear, certainly without fail; packages are whisked to one's home within the time a single rotation of the Earth on its axis occurs. A baseball mitt, high-heeled shoes, crystals with healing properties, a book of poetry, diapers, vitamins, food for pet iguanas—disseminated from factories, products hurl to their destination, pushed by conveyor belts and human toil. Not ironically, this is one of the extenuating factors of the ghosted quality of social life. A person notices the Holy Mary in a fogged mirror; Jesus appears as burnt toast; other apparitions are evoked in haloed light, prismatic and wondrous, signs that disrupt mechanical time's relentlessness. The sun has 330,000 times more mass than the Earth; light is sacred, light is powerful. Light is the result of gases incinerating light years from Earth. Apparitions are illuminations caused by the sun, the sustainer of life. The sun promotes flora and fauna to thrive. The sun powers the machines. Humanity has crushed the sun's rotation into minutes, into seconds and nanoseconds, instituting rushedness.

Because I had retreated to the forest to bury the dog, a dignified protocol, I missed my appointments and now I am delinquent. I had not appeared where I should have been. My trustworthiness and accountability are in jeopardy.

Prisons are filled with first offenders. Time evaporates behind bars. Persons pine away in tightly sealed cells devoid of daylight. Violence is the nature of a system that doesn't prize daylight. Violence is the nature of a culture that is punitive toward life. Dissenters are thrown in prison. The fines are impossible, and prison is inevitable. Total compliance is what the system demands. Exhaustion and depression weigh down on aspects of the soul. Persons pound and drift.

I arrive at the office with forms, deliver them, and thank the workers. We realize we are the clientele, the target audience, the consumers. We lament our plight. Just as the thick steel vault door was closing, a hurricane rips through the building, tearing off the roof. It is mayhem. We run. Adrenaline kicks in. Our veins pump cortisol, activating our sympathetic nervous system. Hail falls in crystal chunks, the roads surge with rushing water. People succumb to the flow. Rescue crews haven't appeared. Our friend Mina was sentenced to twenty-eight days in prison along with other water protectors seeking climate justice and fighting colonial oppression on unceded indigenous lands. The earth is outfitted with artificial arteries; pipelines carrying tar, sands, oil. The eschatological senses rev up. What we really are doesn't have to survive. Insight from YouTube videos. Quit one's status. Become a forest dweller. Pain accesses insights.

I'm in a tree which I've climbed, and my feathers are ruffled. I'm confused about where I am, when I am, who I am. A different cosmology emerges. Feathers drift through the disturbed air, changing colors in the light. Feathers tinged in blood and feathers crusted in ash. Trees within trees and eyes within eyes. Ten thousand stars and ten thousand galaxies.

One disaster compounds another disaster and memory can't account for the chronology of ecological fallout. The head of the agrochemical conglomerate says, "I have one god, how many do you have?" and the organic farmer with a sweeping gesture says, "As many as you see trees all around."

There is a parable too, about impossibility and desire: *eros ton adynaton*, the tale of a man who was called Herbicide and his partner, Bitchazilla. Their real estate venture consisted of flipping buildings. Their company name was called *FlipFlop*. They'd buy buildings that were under market value, often foreclosures, and paint the interiors bright white, add a sink, add a dishwasher, add a shower—inexpensive fixes that they then exorbitantly tallied. They created tiny bedrooms out of medium-sized bedrooms they subdivided. They worked at a frenetic pace, dictating to others the work they wanted done and by when. They operated in a few towns, buying the fixer-uppers wholesale. When there were clusters of cheap homes, they bought them in a lot and razed them, converting the land for a superstore or a minigolf course, whatever the market would bear. They had a reputation, and the townspeople mostly had overlooked the properties they worked on. Eventually all the affordable homes were converted to less-affordable instruments. Herbicide and Bitchazilla, however, lived in a McMansion on the outskirts of town. Their house had twenty gables, three decks, and a star-viewing skylight that was the shape of a star and had taken an outsized crane to mount. But anyway, they had their business, and several other businesses besides, as they flipped buildings morning till night. Their teams worked so fast and expediently that they'd seal scraps of wood and waste material within the walls of the renovation. Cheaper than hauling to the town landfill that charged per pound to dump and didn't accept toxic materials like paint and solvents. The people who worked for Herbicide and Bitchazilla were paid horribly, and often were forced out of their houses that then too were flipped.

Tensions were mounting. Aggression was palpable. Herbicide, who oversaw the relandscaping, experienced doubt that presented itself as an ethical quandary. A man, in Manor Township, had pointed his hand in a gesture resembling a firearm at him. The man was promptly arrested; video surveillance was everywhere and the act didn't pass without notice by local officials. The man had a history of confrontations, and Herbicide, who had thick skin, nevertheless couldn't sanction a sign leveled at him that indicated death.

The incident gave Herbicide a moment of pause. That and that the local Home Depot was out of RoundUp, and so he had to wait twenty-four hours to resupply his lawn crew. He sat in a cafe and pondered. He thought about sitting at the local bar and pounding shots but was too distracted. Bitchazilla sent him unending text messages attempting to keep him on task. He was starting to imagine himself as a caricature of a stereotype in a low-grade horror film that represented the banality of contemporary life, a spectacle he had entered without resistance.

Strangely enough, one afternoon Bitchazilla's texts ceased. There was an email invitation to a gender reveal party for his partner's best friend's baby, otherwise his inbox was quiet. It was the middle of the afternoon on a scorching day when work would seem to halt under sheer exhaustion and dehydration. Everyone crowded around food carts nourishing themselves. Some of the workers were passed out in their cars, the upholstery off-gassing into their vehicles.

Herbicide couldn't keep up with all the worksites so mostly his staff would take breaks to preserve their health and autonomy when they could. He slumped over his lunch. Today was the day to access the Akashic records. Who would have known. His life was never going to be the same. Here he was, forlorn, despondent, feeling bummed out. So close to the light, though overall, disconnected from it. He took a last sip of acidic coffee. A last breath of dull oxygen intake. Marking the occasion when the lost person finds facial recognition in everything living around them, a bird flew by and disappeared into a refraction of glass. For the first time in however long he could remember, he began sobbing.

He had questions about his attachment to amnesia as it relates to social violence. He wasn't mindful. He wasn't here. He wasn't in the past or the future. He wasn't even floating. He was incongruous and sunk. His heart palpitated. Infinite possibilities floated by. He was daydreaming. He found himself selecting the red fruits from the fruit bowl. The bird flew back and winked at him. Elliptical, symmetrical faces once obscured were winking! The sky broke. A thunderstorm kicked up the wind. The bird slapped against the cafe window. He raced outside and recovered the bird. Instinctively he wrapped the bird in a napkin and drove to a veterinary hospital he knew outside of town. He was nowhere to be seen all afternoon. He didn't check in with his staff the next day. He didn't go home. He didn't inform his partner that he would be sleeping in his SUV. She didn't text or call to find out where he was. He wasn't a missing person because no one cared to check in on him. His external world was a habitat of masked information on a highway heading to a strip mall that had closed a decade past. He was in the cafe on the highway's edge that continued to persist thanks to the homey atmosphere exuded by its waitresses and waiters.

This strip mall. This edge of the highway. *Can I drive out of here?* he wondered.

The right brain, dogmatic, logical. The left brain, whimsical, imaginative. Limbs stiff. Leg muscles slack. A tingling electrical impulse under the sole of his foot. His scalp was sweating like a baby's. The usual somatic attention to the groin area, gone. No sensation at his midriff. Something about his neck, taunt and coiled, impulses running through from brain to gut and back under the surface of skin. Signals alerting his hypothalamus. History transforms in the hands of the organizer.

I hope you are having an amazing day and are feeling fine. Thanks for this juicy, sweet fruit salad. I can't describe what is before me verbatim but suffice it to say that there are snakes in the grass, and it is an excellent sign. Caught in a cycle with a glare as red as blood rubies. There is no specific path that snakes take, slithering S's into the underbrush. Reptilian brains. At the speed of sound and at the speed of light, rendered into record. He laughs. Mood instability. Mood alterations. Serpents in the grass. Knowledge. A steep ledge is a precipice. The bird survives. The veterinarian sutures its wing. The bird will rest overnight at the clinic. Herbicide is overtired but feeling different, in a good way. Both he and the bird. The bird, a female mourning dove. Feeling serpentine. Lithe. No inhibition. Fight or flight. Both. Merged.

I can feel my lungs eroding, tiny mountain ranges crumbling, and that give way to cosmic relief, raising suspicion—the vegetal elegance of death and consumption, the fungal audacity of eternal composting.

Shadow self: shadow self.

The image presents itself as a necrosis, an attempt at sickness but the gradations of luminosity block my view.

During the migration, the geese honk and honk and in the background; you can still see the flames and the smoke yet they keep flying forward.

In the tree, I feel like a hanging installation, a nominal and porous being. What are these symptoms of the flesh that cause me to break out so easily? I realize I've been scratching at my arms for several minutes and the red marks on my arms reveal a choreography of irritation and sensitivity. A dance between perimeters of being.

Ok, ok, I mentioned the disasters but how do we get out of this? How do *I* get out of this?

The movements, as if they have been choreographed, as if they have been practiced before. Running and running away and posturing and retreating and yelling aggressively. I have made all of these movements before. I have been making them my entire life. An exemplary model of humanity. Like a perfectly trained dance troupe. I'm clumsy on my feet and trip over cracks in the sidewalk, but in this other waltz, here I am, an experienced showgirl in the montage of attack/retreat, attack/retreat.

A diorama of smoke.

Inhale, inhale, inhale.

Exhale.

Today, I'm optimistic about my ability to chew. In a dream, I tried to find the party but got lost. Instead, there were apples I was going to send as invitations to all my friends, but then the apples were taken and eaten. Still, I realized the messages were sent telepathically and that I would still receive their responses on my phone.

Offering a demand, a white wall, a smile. Smile more often. One syllable at a time. My teeth remember chewing, chewing flesh, chewing meat. What am I craving?

A young environmental activist from a European nation-state arrived on the shore of the harbor and instantly reporters greeted her. She had sailed across an ocean body in a high-tech racing vessel with her father, arriving in time for a global summit on climate change. At sixteen years of age, she garnered attention for her role in spurring on the youth of the world to take action on environmental issues. Every Friday she skipped school to stand in front of Parliament where she held up a sign saying, "School Strike for Climate." Student strikes began appearing all over the globe.

In a front yard in a major city, an important member of the community was murdered in the cold morning light. Chainsaws dug into their flesh. Their midriff was dug into with chains and a crew climbed to their crown. It was a Saturday like any other day. I'm telling you. I was inside looking upon the scene, anticipating it. I then left my apartment and headed closer to what was happening. We crowded around, sickened in our stomachs, heart sickness displacing air. Revolt. Our silent friend (because our hearing was for loud noises) was being dismembered limb by limb. The noise was deafening. The screams of machines meeting living tissue. This morning, a long way from sanity. I should have thrown myself at the men. I should have clung to the tree. The neighbors awaking to the sound of destruction emailed frantically back and forth. Why? A human decision has cascading influence. The effects are threatening. Everyday removal of sentient life. Where will the birds roost? How will we breathe? How will we process sunlight? How will our stories include the storied tree's intelligence? Everyone is stressed. We startle each other with our violence. With our care. Read my mind. This anger becomes a flame that ignites a war. Logic rages against reason. A pitted war of symmetries. One email stated that we were doomed. One stated that all they want is daylight streaming on their mega-porch. Who knows the other's whim? In a strange logic, the bottom branches were spared. The entire crown was decapitated. Just the bottom branches clung to the severed trunk. Birds circled the tree afraid to land, estranged by the changes. The tree was the oldest member of the community. Other trees in this community of trees had succumbed to a cyclone that tore through the yards some years past. The vibrations of the tree in its compromised state tore through consciousness.

Smile in the face of disaster.

Then you turn a lever. Then a word. In a painful fashion.

We just kept on listening.

I didn't see.

A list of the dog hairs that I didn't see but saved in my pocket.

The list in my pocket.

Just like that, with no memory of the consequences, blinking out of turn. Pass it around. Pass it around.

From inside the climate summit, a gathering of world leaders listened as the young climate activist began her call to action. She didn't flinch. Her posture was confident, and she conveyed passionate fury.

This is wrong. I shouldn't be up here. I should be back in school on the other side of the ocean, yet, you come to us young people for hope, how dare you!

You have stolen my dreams and my childhood with your empty words and yet I'm one of the lucky ones.

People are suffering. People are dying. Entire ecosystems are collapsing. We are in the beginning of a mass extinction. And all you can talk about is money and fairy tales of eternal economic growth.

How dare you!

For more than thirty years the science has been crystal clear. How dare you continue to look away and come here saying that you are doing enough when the politics and solutions needed are still nowhere in sight.

You said you hear us. And that you understand the urgency, but no matter how sad and angry I am I do not want to believe that, because if you really understood the situation and still kept on failing to act, you would be evil, and I refuse to believe.

The popular idea of cutting our emissions in half in ten years only gives us a 50% chance of staying below 1.5 degrees and the risk of setting off irreversible chain reactions beyond human control. 50% may be acceptable to you, but those numbers do not include tipping points, most feedback loops, additional warming hidden by air pollution and the aspects of equity and climate justice. They also rely on my generation sucking 100s of billions of tons of your CO2 out of the air with technologies that barely exist. So, a 50% risk is simply not acceptable to us when you have to live with the consequences. To have a 67% chance of staying below a 1.5 degree of global temperature rise—the best odds given by the IPCC—the world has 420 gigatons of CO2 left to emit, back in January 1, 2018. Today that figure is already down to less than 350 gigatons.

How dare you pretend that this can be solved with business as usual and some technological solutions?

With today's emissions levels, that remaining CO2 budget will be entirely gone within less than 8½ years.

There will not be any solution or plans presented in line with these figures here today because these numbers are too uncomfortable, and you are still not mature enough to tell it like it is. You are failing us, but the young people are starting to understand your betrayal. The eyes of all future generations are upon you, and if you choose to fail us, I say we will never forgive you. We will not let you get away with this. Right here right now is when we draw the line, and change is coming whether you like it or not. Thank you!

Outside the United Nations, where the Climate Action Summit

was taking place, Kayapó Tribe Chief Raoni Metuktire, whose home is the Amazon rainforest, spoke with reporter Nermeen Shaikh. Later, when attempting to enter the proceedings, he was denied passage.

Today there are many things happening in Brazil. In the previous government it wasn't like this, it wasn't so bad. Now the Bolsonaro government is authorizing deforestation, he's authorizing the entrance of wild cat miners and loggers and mining companies into indigenous territories. This is bad because it will destroy everything. It will destroy the forest. Destroy the Amazon. It will be bad for us in the future. This is what I defend. I don't defend standing virgin forests just for me—no, I'm thinking of the future, our grandchildren, and great-grandchildren, living in peace in this forest, so what Bolsonaro is doing is very bad for me.

Do you have any hope that something will happen at this summit? Bolsonaro is not here. President Trump is in the building, but he's not attending the climate summit. What do you hope will happen to save the Amazon here, if anything?

I hope that something good comes out of this gathering. I hope that they decide to help the Amazon and the environment. I hope that here, in this gathering, they help the Amazon to remain. This is what I want. I don't want people to be in conflict. We need to live in peace, to live well, to live without conflict. This is what I think. I always say this, and this is what I say now, this is my thinking: for you to hear that we should live in peace without fights, without problems, without conflicts. This is what I think.

And what are indigenous groups like your own people doing to resist Bolsonaro's policies in the Amazon?

We Kayapó want to continue defending our lands, our forests, our future, and our people. We will resist. We will continue — I will continue speaking so they in Brazil will respect us, that they respect our culture, our customs, our land. I've been saying this and I'm saying it again, here, but destruction is happening around our area. Soy and corn planters are destroying all of the forest surrounding our land but we, Kayapó will resist, we will continue our struggle to not have invasions of miners, loggers, fishermen. This is what I do not like and do not accept.

You said the Amazon, which we know is very important for the survival of humanity, not just for the community who've lived there. Explain why the Amazon is so important for the climate of the world.

I've seen that the standing forest cools the land, the land becomes cold, becomes normal. If you deforest as we are seeing deforestation, there will be no more trees to provide shade.

The woman stands at the end of the lake, the lake like a finger, one finger of many fingers of many hands. She ponders the view. The view for which so many will destroy and pay for. What is the value of the view of a body of water? Why are we so attracted to these wells of natural wisdom, and yet are willing to destroy so much of what binds it to us in an effort to capture it, own it, possess it? The appeal is that it cannot be possessed. And yet, we must possess it. This is what is at stake.

She watches the water ripple and hit the rocks, feels the cold wind and the spittle of the lake on her face. Here she can see the direct and cosmic influence of the universe, in the movement of the water, the molecular interconnectedness of the entire universe, the utter entanglement of worlds and Worlds and worlding, all in those tiny cold drops of water that hit her face.

It is cold, she thinks. *I've never felt more alive*, she thinks. *And yet, I am dying*, she thinks. *And—*

Another list, of things that may be done on purpose, or how it is that we hope to change, or what was witnessed by one singular squirrel over a course of many rainy afternoons:

- Arms, like spokes on a wheel, rapidly turning, picking up speed, *vroom vroom* sounds emanating from the compact body. This may also be referred to as the process of adaptation.
- The word "problem" gets repeated and thrown around by the humans as if there are "problems," as if there are "problems to be solved," as if there are "solutions," rather than constant becomings. Aren't we all changelings? Aren't we all forever shapeshifting from one state to another, even death as another state we will pass into, just to begin anew?
- Mushrooms sprouting up overnight after the rain. Mushrooms covered over by falling leaves. Mushrooms growing

up through the leaves and then human feet trampling and kicking over the mushrooms. Mushroom shards left on the sidewalk, fungal chunks of growth and rot. This may also be referred to as "human intention."

- Geese flying overhead in a V and then two stragglers honking more loudly than the rest. More honking from a distance. Balance of wings and water. This is how we can understand what we are even doing here.

"We all have the capacity to heal each other—healer is a possibility in each of us... Healing is the resilience instinct of our bodies."

adrienne maree brown's words reverberated in her. The world became more apparent. The dimensions of light and dark interpenetrated her. Dark energy and the light spectrum merging in blood and bone. A color changed from peachy orange into crepuscular red, and somehow into black. Black rocks, black cosmic expanse, black letters of words conjured in the mind's eye. The colors varied as they drained into her mind. Leaves fell on her head, littered her torso. Deciduous trees are able to collect sunlight for half of the year, maybe a bit more, and then they shed their coats, stand erect, nude in the wind, withstanding the storms. She stripped down and merged with the lake. Out of season, the lake was colder than an unheated room, colder than the inside of a refrigerator, the vegetable bin. She opened up the lake as it closed around her. The lake posed no resistance and no attachment; she could glide in as easily as she could again extract herself from the frigid waters, yet it held her in suspension. The liquid of her body neutralized in the liquid of the lake. Vessel within vessel. The dogma of consciousness slipped out of her. Received ideas turned to gas and floated outside of her. She was clear liquid and also bone marrow darkness. The lake lapped against her sensitivities. The metaphor of crisis and the reality of crisis met up in bone space. She felt she had no control over the water of the lake. No control. The water, though, had an influence on her. She did have some control. Indeed, she did. Political objects waged a war in her thinking apparatus. She was again ensconced within an environmental holism. The conditions were identical. Was this lake here, in this environment, when she was a kid? Did geological forces produce this lake? How could she reimagine human capacity by giving over identity to a lake? She must be available for her ally, this lake.

When you ignore the suffering of others, you don't understand the world. That's a basic fact of ethics. If others are suffering, there can't be oblivion. She submerged her skull under the weedy water. The brackish debris on top clung to her hair and dragged across her face. Her vision was obscured. Her eyes stung. She felt violent pain as an abstraction and then it located in her neck. It radiated up her skull via the spinal cord. She gasped for breath; her heart accelerated its pulse. Suffering is mostly neither random nor arbitrary. She agreed with a post-colonial anti-racist theorist on this. She was working on an essay that had to do with capacitation and incapacitation. She used her hometown as a case study. A blighted post-industrial town, razed. A blighted post-industrial town of ecological beauty.

She dipped down again, and when she came up to the surface she was breathing sharply. An image of fire. An image of flooding. She swam as fast as she could to the center of the lake until her heart resisted to the point of rapid, erratic thundering. Look into capacitation. Encourage capacitation. Offer the lake one's energy. Remove the plastic objects littering the water and the coast. One world with a wooden frame. Two worlds with infinite galaxies. One vernacular architectural model. Two versions of the system. Sip the water. Respond to the water. The water is responsive. The lake responds. 🦎❀ ⁺✧ˋ(⁰▿⁰)ˊ✧⁺❀

She senses the swelling and leaving of her heart at the bottom of the lake. Makes the journey deep down to retrieve it, another journey deep down to retrieve a part of her soul. The accumulation of living energy. As she releases heaviness, she increases lightness, finds it harder to dive deep down into the depths, feels her body floating naturally toward the surface of the lake, on the surface of the lake, above the surface of the lake, floating upward into the sky, becoming a cloud, dissolving into the sky and the atmosphere and the climate that holds this and everything below, while the lake also ponders—

Above the lake, a much broader view of the lake. Above the lake, dark clouds have enveloped our emotions. Our pain becomes bound up with the torn net entangled in the reeds. Above the lake, a murmuration of starlings fly in a pattern of *everything is possible* and the solemn dance is as magical as it is mundane, is as fantastical as it is initiatory, and the gaps between worlds, as the ever-changing pattern of birds, the negative space in the murmuration, is a shadow murmuration, is just as vibrant, just as dense, just as incited. Above the lake, an alternative view of death; symmetry becomes an illusion, and death, in the form of the wounds of everyone's bitter regret manifests as breath, bird-breath manifests as heightened self-knowledge, knowledge manifests as transformational thrust, and the death rites aren't anything to fear when one is always and already ready for anything. Above the lake, we feel the instinct in our guts as we fly together. I can hear the music, I can hear it, can't you? Above the lake, we remember that life is worth living, and seeing the dancing pattern of us in the water below, I can access a primordial cohesion that feels absurd to have forgotten. Above the lake, the absurdity is the narrow witnessing of an event, events being how we humans measure *happening*, and our preoccupation with awe obscures the magic of mundanity, and that is what all this is really about. Above the lake, the hardest thing to relate to is my own positionality. I want to be in the air, but I don't have the corporeal structure to take flight. I want to be in the water, but I don't know how to swim and am afraid that I will drown. I want to be someone else, but the laws of physics prevent me from assuming another identity. Except that none of that is true. I make excuses with my expert rationality and there is always a reason why something isn't possible. I can't. I mean, I cannot. And yet the pattern reminds me of my own foolishness. I only need to close my eyes and imagine it all into reality. I breathe out from my mouth to be in the air, there alongside the starlings. I breathe out from my heart to feel the sensation of being enveloped by water, the warmth of fluidity and smothering, of utter and complete support. I breathe out from my belly and I am already who I imagine myself to be. But can I trust this? Can I trust myself?

The lake and the lake above the lake revive my consciousness so that my consciousness receives direct information from all forms of life that pulsate simultaneously as one interrelational current. The lake within me and the lake, as an external property of lakes, all together, pulsate. I become the lake, and the lake becomes that which I am, and all my relatives are an extension of a family of lakes, as are all of my deceased ancestors. Water is a major component of my nature, my architecture. Look now how watery my eyes become as they stare at the surface tension of the lake. Look how my legs disappear into the water as if the water were consuming me, intimately all-knowing. The lake allows me to withdraw myself from their viscous depths as I allow the lake to withdraw from me as a singular principle, momentarily arising as a lake or as a rain shower or as a cyclone spooled with torrents of water. The earth's consistency is water, wind, fire, and soil. I vaguely recall the feeling of the lake sucking up the detritus of the shore in a rush of emotion and then, months later, my mother giving birth to me in a gush of embryonic fluid that poured out of her and onto the floor. I was sticky with viscous fluid, a lake bursting forth. My mother birthed me as a replication of lakes. She is a replication of lakes. I am a replication of lakes. Lakes are replications of oceans and clouds are replications of oceans. When I was born, my mother was duplicated and this duplication, me, transformed her form into a difference that both resembled and denied her and the lake from which we originated.

My distant relations—my greatest grandparents are hazy figments of my imagination. I can see their resemblance in water, in plants, in minerals, in fauna. I can look at an exacting genetic portrait of these ancestors in the present. In a lab I can begin to understand their components. The lake and the river and the ocean ushered in personhood and my distant relations are your distant relations and we are all lakes, rivers, and oceans. Luca is the name of our earliest ancestor and their code lives within us. Luca is never more than one step removed from contemporary life.

When my mother's womb released fluids that spilled onto the floor, the fluids joined the continuum of wetness that fills life with moisture and sustains the vascular circuitry of veins. Everyone remarked how I resembled my father, a lake, and my mother, a river. I drink copious amounts of water, always require moisture.

I was told that a squirrel hurled a nut at the sun and demanded that the sun highlight the occasion of watery fluids giving rise to sentient life. The squirrel in this iteration was a hologram. Potentiality was contained in the water and in the sun. The two had to intersect, they had to create a bond. In the gullies and the divots, murky water gathered and microorganisms by the name Luca harnessed energies. This occurred far after oceanic formations, as gas and liquid molecules were agitated in swimming gestures. The oceans, with moon sway, moved in motion and the molecules responded by bonding and propelling through the washy mass of waves.

Luca defies history by being blurred within a terrestrial story. Luca, the sun calls, and everyone who has a circulatory system is made to respond. We all tilt orifices toward the sun. The sway of motion causes changes in the wind pattern. Luca is a circadian progenitor of our mother. Swallow some saliva and reactivate Luca as they travel to the gut.

Water evaporates in fire. This state change is epic. Now is a time of fire within a time of water as locked snow on epic peaks melt, causing monumental flooding.

Gradually, we begin to understand the basic needs of fire and the basic needs of water and where they deviate, and an administrative code of conduct arises.

Luca, come forward and speak to us in the present tense. You do, you always do. You are here, everywhere. You manage to stay relevant, to speak the language of the present. You are the last universal common ancestor. You've encrypted time into all of us.

In the lake, I bond with you, Luca, and see myself as a liquid mirror slick and orbital.

Luca, we have much to discuss as a form of living. We are shifting, but are we regressing? We know the answer. Lines are tangled. We awaken in entanglement.

Already, you've got your head in the clouds. Already, you know that water is not a border, and in our weightlessness we will create new channels for crying and sweating, our snot running together in the everything that is us, our tears as memory, leaking through the unprecedented sight we gesture with. Seeing is a gesture, leaking memory is a gesture, and we resist domestication through the fluidity of our forms.

Don't you remember being a cloud, floating above the cities and the forests, your progeny floating past and leaking moisture to rain down on the worlds below? Don't you remember the gestures of dust particles, in every moment noticing an exchange in spite of what darkens, gaining momentum because uncertainty is what causes the tremors in your fingers, and there was that one day that you fell so profoundly and hit the ground with the greatest of thuds? Don't you remember being poured into a stone cup, exiled from the sky but still a part of that elevated kingdom, everything and everything, and yet—don't you remember floating out there in space among the stars, surprised at the fullness of it all, all of your emotions captured in the traces of moisture that were wiped off my cheek when I remembered you, when I longed for you, when I felt you in my bones, in my organs, in between each ligament and metacarpal, and when I felt you in the weightless wombs of fluidic possibility. I was still there to reach out for you because the reaching is important, more important than anything else perhaps, even more important than the idea. I remember it all, do you?

She had stumbled within the construction site, banging into unstable scaffolding holding heavy equipment that had slid off the metal shelving onto her cranium. One side of her head was bleeding as she lay slumped under the debris inside a kind of makeshift closet. Mute in her unconsciousness, she lay undetected. The closet was really a built-out section of the newly constructed building that was being covered and subsumed into the design. The last of the sheet rock was assembled around her as her still form remained beneath toppled tubs of plaster and a broken saw that someone had neglected to throw away; the saw had been cast aside along with other broken tools in an area of the structure that was being enclosed. The deadline for the building's completion was tight; there was pressure to have it finished. The outer walls went up around her as she remained motionless and oblivious. No one suspected she was there. The wheezing of nail guns on the wall's exterior did not revive her.

Only later, after the workers had left and she was in total darkness, did she come to. She was encased in darkness. The seams of the sheetrock had been completed which meant she was sealed airtight within dimensions the size of a tiny closet. A sense of panic arose in her. Her cell phone had no reception. She had been abandoned behind the walls of her investment property that she and her partner were having constructed. Once revived, she realized her predicament, and she began to think of ways to release herself, but her legs couldn't fully stretch so she couldn't kick at the wall sufficiently and she knew punching the concrete sheetrock would do nothing. Still, she pounded with her fists, but no one heard her. It was the beginning of the weekend, and she was trapped without food and water in a nearly airtight capsule. She screamed and then burst into sobs, and as her body shuddered, a menacing realization invaded the space, invading her muscles and nerves. She became cold and without feeling. Her sense of time dissipated. Waves of hunger came and went; thirst dominated her thoughts. She scrounged around in her bag but all she had were her phone, pens, and lipstick. Nothing to address the parchedness.

At one point she dozed off. When she gained consciousness she went through a similar cycle of panic, disbelief, confusion, and desperation. The tight dark space became chilly and her muscles seized. She banged some more but realized it must be the middle of the night.

A new day began. She was inside the cell-like space, cramped, and distraught. She'd had to defecate and now sat in the corner as far away from the emission, overwhelmed by what was happening to her. She searched for a sharp object to burrow into the concrete walls. A pen was all she could come up with. She began to etch a divot into the wall. The wall was impervious. She took off a shoe and began banging against the wall. It shuddered but didn't crack or give way. Finally, after what must have been hours of activity, she again slumped over and slept off her frustration.

Some time had passed, it must have been the latter part of day two when she perceived smoke. At first the smoke was a blessing, a sensation emanating from beyond her confines. She was aroused by the scent of burning. The light wisps of smoke seemed to warm the air and diffuse the chemical smell of concrete and building materials that gassed off around her. The smoke was light and didn't cause her anxiety at first. Again, she had to relieve herself and this time it wasn't as humiliating or monstrous to let fluids and waste pour out of her. She submitted to the pressure of her bowels and, after squatting in the corner, she felt somewhat restored.

The smoke got thicker as it became a material presence. It ghosted her. It was an amorphous visitation of the outside world. She coughed and wheezed. She fidgeted in her cell. She restricted her breath and then gasped for air. Normally, she never considered breath, breathing. Now she was fixated on it. She couldn't get her breathing rhythm in sync. Initially she felt certain it wasn't the building she was in that was going up in flames, the smoke was too light, but she began to doubt her perceptions. She redoubled the frenzied thinking and in her mind's eye scanned the landscape around the periphery of the building. Trees, stretches of fields, a river. The superstore under construction; she and her partner were the principal investors. She was trapped within their speculative venture. Adjacent to the superstore, another monolith—a data center. The data center, could it be what was on fire? The data center was unlikely to catch on fire and burn for long—alarms would ring. Its machinery was cooled continually by water from the river. It was a highly monitored operation and had a sensitive alarm system in place. She didn't hear any alarms. The smoke was getting to her. She was faint. Nauseous. Her cough was a hacking that thudded against the resilient walls. Hours passed.

She was stiff and cold and numb. Not yet senseless but heading into that mental and physical zone. She had come by to inspect the building before heading out for the holidays. The site would be quiet until after the New Year.

Time entered her nervous system, her circulatory system, her DNA. Time congealed as a cellular present ebbing toward an unknown future. Without natural light there was no regulation of time except her gut that told her she was hungry and her circadian rhythm told her she was tired. She had no more discharge to relieve herself of. She was emptied out. Time was fading within her while becoming increasingly dynamic around her. She was dizzy and out of sorts. She took off her clothing, and with her clothing she made herself a nest.

She slept and her eyes crusted over. Her skin was sticky. Her crotch stuck to the sweater she sat on. The smoke became a pillow of softness that soothed her.

Had days passed? She wasn't sure. She chewed on the pink patterned handle of her purse as if it were jerky. As she masticated the leather it became soft. She swallowed. Immediately she vomited the substance. She realized she had been chewing a snake that had died to make the purse. Under what circumstance? Where, she wondered? Where did the snake originate?

The smoke wrapped itself around her like a veil. Her memory seemed to be represented by smoke.

I was hemmed in within walls of silence. Screams were remote in the echo chamber of my chaos. The sheetrock muffled my urgent decibels. I sweated profusely, then my body gave way to fevered chills. I maintained a crouching position because it was the only posture possible within the confines of the subwalls that encased me. I had been unconscious when the walls were built up around me. There was a tarpaulin thrown over some broken debris and I used it as a blanket when I realized I was trapped. The confines numbed me. My survival instincts were slow to kick in. My thoughts were fragments of hard mineral, deep within a mine shaft, unrefined crude formulations.

There aren't even screams to be heard. Already already already.

She remembered things from her life one moment at a time. To remember a moment in a day, a life in the world realized. Trees, over.

As she limped around the chamber thinking on what waited for her outside of the building, the tension throbbed in the memory of the building, the importance of the debris, of what she could remember still.

Hemmed in, an exchange of chaos. The darkness. She—darkness. Darkness, me. There was the seeing of black halves, randomly stoned to thirst, thrown, and unstable in the head. It wasn't so crude, her form, but the screams radiated and bled into what she considered was herself. Action was seeing, neglect was the skin being unkind.

She scrounged like someone who had come by the crude form of her selfhood, molten already, and remembered again coming by the workers. She had no knowledge of waste materials, gassing, what they were gassing. The future.

She now sat and one day began. She sweated it off. When she vomited the deadline, she knotted her fingers and felt the trepidation of uncertainty—what caused her to formulate any of this? She couldn't fully stretch out the capacity of fluidic possibility, so she lay slumped and distraught. Was this all a repeat? Was she stuck in some sort of looping? No one suspected. Wave of smoke. Inhalation awoke her body, shuttered up, subsumed in the human's own weightlessness, wombs of an unknown, for they could come up with more walls within the walls, a wall, and a walled womb. Shuttered.

But the superstore. Always a superstore. Had she ever wondered where she would sleep at night? Tonight: the cloud floating, a senseless womb of smoke. At first the womb in the subwalls became like hunger assembling in the confines of her belly, broken debris like thoughts of depravity, and she used whatever water she could find, squatting, poured into the tree rings. Trees: stretch and stuck to the parched air. She was a wall of sorts, wasn't she? She had passed on the question; an answer would not revive itself. The smoke of clouds. Already she felt thicker and was still bleeding. What was imminent? What was invading her breath?

She struggled with the notion of subterranean worlds. Her snot revived her corporeal sense of being, but in reality, it was her breath that was invading the sky and her thoughts, like time receptors; her legs couldn't fully stretch, stuck to the air and outer walls and she fidgeted with it all, everything and diffuse and happening and present and ebbing, and she couldn't hear what was being told to her. Nothing. Not anymore.

Part of her body broke off, or broke in two. She was her body and then her body became a figment, a veil, a gap—plus something, minus something. Yet she was able to access her history, her stories. She was suddenly able to access different feelings, somatic sensations. Her breath canvassed the ceiling and then through tiny gaps in surface tension, was able to escape and thus canvas the sky. For a while, breath was the entirety of being. Breath was seen through water vapor that had circulated within her body. An expended gas, a byproduct of her lungs. The breath that she emitted was quickly reabsorbed by the trees and plants outside the renovation site. The trees and plants sensed her presence. They converted her breath into generative gasses that became intake into her circulatory system. The tempo of her dispersion was slow. Her breath was slowing. The breath that left her body was a little cloud of consciousness that delivered messages of her bodily status. Floating where the wind made them drift, these breaths eventually settled.

Part of her body became inert. She melted into a form and then the form solidified. This took hours of cellular rearrangement. As her breath departed so did her spirit, through a blooming exit in her forehead, a portal for energized presences. This different impression of her was a matter of different form. She drifted and partook in the wind's currents. As she vacated her body and merged with the atmosphere, thinking lost its objectives. The day was rainy, and the water coursed through her. She remained elevated above the earth as vapor. Freely, contingency hybridized body within body within thought within feeling. There was no loss of consciousness, only changes in form.

Parts of her earthly energy fell in the form of condensation onto the gigantic metal roof of the superstore. Parts of her, in the form of water droplets that clung to the atmosphere of her breath, trickled into a small pond by the edge of the highway. Tall reeds drank the energized waters. A small rodent sank its teeth into the tall reed's roots, enjoying her traces.

When her corpse was found, after a comprehensive search finally had pinpointed her whereabouts in the tiny closet of the building, an obituary was written. Work on the building halted. The building became a crime scene and was taped off and demolished in sections to understand better what her body was doing behind the walls.

Articles in the press began to probe the connection between the woman, the partially constructed superstore, and the data center. Her financial footprint became public knowledge. The fact of her entombment within the unfinished building greatly disturbed the residents of the town, and a fact-finding mission was underway.

Somehow her partner, Herbicide, was out of the picture. Had he left town? No one was sure. Their joint assets were frozen until the investigation concluded. Why he wasn't a prime suspect was curious. The workers were questioned initially, but it was clear they had nothing to do with the circumstances. Ultimately, the case was closed.

The land that the superstore and the data center occupied was once one continuous parcel. Recently, Bitchazilla and Herbicide had purchased a part of the parcel of land to build the superstore.

They purchased the tract with the profits made from transactions of foreclosed and undervalued real estate in the town and surrounding districts, buying and flipping investments. The superstore and the data center shifted the town's focus from that of small-scale farms that produced enough food for local consumption to cloud computing and, soon following, cheap home goods. It is true, many residents drove a considerable distance to a superstore in a neighboring town to access such products. Shopping at superstores seemed to be an unavoidable necessity.

The prospects of employment at the superstore and at the data center were, for the most part, minimum wage jobs that necessitated federal government supplementation of worker incomes. Now her breath seeped into the superstore, and customers and workers alike breathed in the vapor of her expended exhalation. The oversized racks of sweatpants on sale by the checkout absorbed the carbon dioxide along with other endogenous, volatile organic compounds originating from her body, biomarkers of her exposure to toxins and pathogens that remained in her system. Dolls with brown hair, blond hair, and black hair absorbed these expirations. Towels and toilet paper, curtains and fabric on rolls absorbed the moisture. The store-goers exhaled and inhaled in a rhythmic pulse as the day unraveled in time and space.

As a revenant, she lost judgement and was now total existence. She drifted in tandem with drift. She was part of wind, and then moist and dewy. She was the shiny slick sheen on a teddy bear's plastic eyes and also the condensation on a prepackaged six-pack of pudding. She caused bird seed to become moldy and cheeses to turn green. Her manifestation as a foggy atmosphere created a subtle haze that fogged up car windshields. She was swampy and also dried crusty onto sneakers and was trekked into living rooms. Dogs who rolled in the mud at the dog parks and cats who licked their dog companions sensed her. She landed in the gut of the dog and the gut of a cat and the gut of a squirrel and was as volatile as combustible gas.

I was consumed by the world as I consumed the world.

After the time at the lake when I experienced a kind of reckoning, I felt different within myself and different about what existed around me. Ions realigned. Change at the tiniest level. I felt disposed toward simple chores. Mundane gestures. The small mechanical functions of life. I'd be doing the dishes and images would flood my mind. Shimmering light. A hazy horizon line. Visual cues that gave me direct information about the future. Yet, the past seemed to be what was relevant. It became obvious to me that my mind now tended to focus on a distant past instead of an immediate past. A distant past I didn't realize I had experienced. Information about the distant past streamed in. Why was I conjuring a scenario that took place outside my purview? Let me be clear, these weren't historical events of my lifeline I was processing. Yet they were...

VIRUS

In that winter, distance was about to shrink in scope. What appeared far away became zoomed in on. What was close at hand was also miles and miles elsewhere. A mutuality of experience was beginning to occur for residents of Earth.

West breathed in the East. The South absorbed the North. Movement on the sphere created a vacuum.

The time was the beginning of 2020. The time was new and different. The time was continuum and motion. Burying the past created friction in the future.

The smallest elements claimed attention.

What are the kinds of scenes we see in this newly lifted poultice? What is the soreness that is lifted, replaced, dissolved, in question?

A scene:

> A birch tree.
> The bark peels off like strips of paper.
> "Is it dying?" A child asks.
> "No, why do you say that?"
> "Paper comes from dead trees."

A scene:

> "Is that a bone or twig?"
> "What's the difference?"

The child doesn't know to ask for evidence. In truth, the child holds a feather and can feel the weight in her palm but doesn't know how to measure the weight in grams. The wind is speaking to her, she knows this, but she doesn't yet know what is being said, though she feels a response rising in her belly.

The squirrels were all sharpening their teeth yesterday. Today they are quiet.

The child isn't sure if the feeling rising in her belly is hunger or a response for the wind, or another question masked by the digestive juices intermingling with curiosity.

The routines are different. The parks are closed, and the playgrounds are locked up. Mother and father might be working from home now, or mother and child are still on the street sheltering from the elements. Everyone begins to wear masks. People distance themselves from one another. Instead of eating together in a large cafeteria, she and her mom now go to a place to pick up a bag of food from a restaurant. The squirrels are in exactly the places she always sees them. They look back at her gaze with acorns in their mouths. They savor the nuts and seeds they buried in the fall, now while the food supply is low. She walks with her mother back to the overpass and they sit and eat sandwiches that the restaurant distributed. In the city in which they live it is cold, but not freezing. She asks her mom the meaning of a word like "north" or a word like "south."

Direction weighed against the feather, weighed against the breath on her palm, weighed against the breath inside the mask. Breath shifting direction to drift off like the dandelion seeds carried off in the wind. Truthful feather in one palm, truthful detritus, or seeds in the other. Tipping over the edge and making sounds with sticks against the bark, messianic bird sounds are carried. From which direction? Backtracking to take flight. Once, she was taught a dance she now could not remember. She feels the movement twitching from inside her right foot.

You were born a green mouse, her mother tells her. *Yes, it is true, a green mouse full of glee.* You ask questions to fill yourself up. What is a question but a prompt, a way to draw the world into your body. *I was sure you were born a green mouse. Look now, you are still a green mouse and as time flows, I'm also convinced that you are becoming a blue heron. How I know this is one thing, it is also for you to find out. My answer will always be incomplete. It is how I see you as part of me, the part of me that has departed yet resides most firmly. A blue heron. And here we are on a curb eating sandwiches in the middle of a pandemic. We must remember to dance.*

To see ourselves for a brief moment, just as we are, of the earth and the questions and the dance. She spins and spins, suddenly remembers the movement, an endless spiral and she pounds her feet into the ground, *to see ourselves,* and she spirals endlessly, *just as we are,* and the squirrels look down at the child spinning, *their noses turned like questions, without pausing the sharpening of their teeth,* and she waves her arms in the air like wings, *the squirrels have other things to worry about today,* and she spins and spins, in that endless spiral, until she becomes the grouse she always was before today and will be when the earth returns to its natural orbit. The virus is looking down at the earth from inside the earth and is looking outward from the child and into the eyes of her mother and the virus spins and spins, remembers the movement, an endless spiral, and pounds into the bodies of others, seeing what is returned, returning what is seen.

Out of the vortex of the center she creates, the girl crashes to the ground. Her mother clasps the child to her chest. The girl looks up at her mother's face which is obscured by the sun. Her face is total light—a hazy aura. The girl feels disoriented by wonder. She asks the light about what she sees. What is happening? How come people are avoiding each other but yet we cling together? Why do we draw closer, and the other people push further away? She recoiled when handed a paper bag of food. The mother places the girl softly on the curb and gets up herself. Begins to spin, slowly and deliberately in a circle. She spins until she is dizzy, she spins until she is nauseous. She whirls and whirls and her orbit is the shape of a cell, the shape of the Earth. Then she stops and she looks at her daughter and asks her daughter if she knows what tomorrow will feel like and of course her daughter says, *of course not, I don't know anything about tomorrow.*

The distancing, they say, is the answer. There are too many of us and we need to stay separated, six feet apart, in brief moments we may catch glimpses and breaths and in those brief moments of intimacy, when we cave to our human inclination for connection, the virus will leap and propagate. The virus is taking advantage of our weaknesses, they say. We must beat it with our persistent nature, the way we always have. By building walls and boundaries and keeping them out. The virus can't outsmart us, they say. We will always find a solution, always one step ahead. It's just a matter of digging deeper, looking deeper into the dust of decay, the dead bodies that disturb the soil and we just need to dig deeper, they say. A small fern emerging from the crevice in the brick wall. A patch of moss under the leaking pipe in the alleyway. Green seedlings shooting up from the spaces in between the building foundation and the sidewalk. The distance, though, is the answer, they insist. Stay away and we will find a cure. They spit on each other and wave hexes in the air. Others cross the street to avoid sharing breath. The distancing, they are screaming now, is the answer. The grouse is still dancing, kicking up all the dust. The dust is getting everywhere, on the moss, on your skin. The dust penetrates your mask, and you breathe it in. The dust can't be controlled because it's the dust from your future dead body coming back to be absorbed. The dust is everywhere. And yet, they say, distancing is the answer.

There are hoarding tendencies and collective tendencies—with mutual aid in mind. Simultaneously both motivations were happening. People who could afford to stockpile groceries and necessary supplies were doing so. Secondary refrigerators sold out. Toilet paper sold out. Major chain stores had difficulty restocking provisions to the shelves. There were also cottage industries forming. People sewing face masks for health care workers and vulnerable members of the community. People distributing food and offering to babysit for the children of first responders. Help was needed everywhere, and one couldn't rely on the State for a feeling of safety or care.

What was this infinitesimally small virus? How could it have such resounding effects on human health? Where did it come from? Was it alive? Why hadn't humanity prepared for such an event? The dust was everywhere, and viruses were everywhere; now viruses were truly everywhere and in everyone.

She could hear the sound, as if a cry, multiplying behind everyone's view. They were all preparing. They were all in the mode of "just in case." Toilet paper is running low! They all respond by buying all the toilet paper. They will kill each other to get the toilet paper. Not enough masks! Recommendation: wear masks! They all respond by buying all the masks. They will kill each other to get the masks. Great quarantine activity: baking bread! They all respond with sourdough starters, baking bread, posting pictures. They will kill each other for the best sourdough pictures, the best loaves in the neighborhood, the best loaves on Instagram, the best loaves in the galaxy. The child and her mother return from the grocery store. The mother takes off their masks and puts them into Ziploc bags and puts them into a Tupperware on the front porch. The mother sprays something that smells onto the child's hands, tells her to rub her hands together. "Sing Happy Birthday," the mother instructs. "I hate that song," the child responds. The mother scowls and a crow caws down the street. The child sings the theme from The Muppet Show instead. "It's the Muppet Show." The mother wipes down the front doorknob. "It's time to play the music." The mother wipes down each item from the grocery bags before putting them away. "It's time to light the lights." The mother folds the paper bags and puts them under the doormat.

"It's time to meet the Muppets on the Muppet Show tonight." The mother washes her hands in the kitchen sink. Her skin is peeling from the dryness. "It's time to put on makeup." The child is still standing outside singing, watching the squirrels having sex in the pear tree. "It's time to dress up right." The mother takes off all of her clothes and puts them in a garbage bag to wash later. "It's time to raise the curtain on the Muppet Show tonight." The mother gets into the shower.

As the mother and daughter were driving home from the store they actually passed the other mother and her daughter, but the two parties didn't see each other. This was typical. Class differences, though glaring, were inconspicuous to many. The mother and her daughter in the car and the mother and the daughter on the curb, semblance. The mother and the daughter who sanitized themselves on their return to safety: to their home, to their sanctuary continued with their day. They baked the perfect loaf of bread! A real achievement. It felt good to do something together in the kitchen, mother and daughter. To enjoy domesticity, as it was duly enforced for health reasons. The mother and daughter out of doors also were talking about bread. They were also enjoying the intimacy of togetherness. They possessed an internal knowledge of the gift that they shared as relation. Now was the time to find a place to shelter. Now was the time to find a place to feel safe. The mother and daughter who didn't have a permanent residence headed to the expanse of woodland and climbed a small hill and they both reclined in the sun. It was a moment of boundless energy and tenderness.

Recipe For Virus-Free Sourdough Bread:

3 bottles hand sanitizer
1 ½ tsp sanitized yeast
1 ½ tsp sanitized salt
2 ½ tsp sanitized flour
2 cups sanitized sourdough starter
½ cup sanitized lukewarm water

Mix all ingredients...

"Mother, this bread tastes like the stuff you spray on my hands."
"It's safe. What you're tasting is safety."
"But I don't want to eat this."
"It's your breakfast. Eat it. It's fresh. I want to post a picture of you eating the bread on Instagram."
"Can I at least have some butter?"
"You have to spray the butter first. And the knife. And your hands."
"I just want to go to bed."
"One photo first."
"Ok."

It is true that life was collapsing into screens and that as screens took precedence dimensionality in all its nuance began to collapse, sort of. Two dimensions can be dangerous to the soul. It is a known fact that if you collapse three dimensions into two dimensions for too long there will be hell to pay. It is tempting to do so and ultimately easy. It appears easy because you can't initially tell what is destroyed in the process. The screen allows distances to grow between bodies. Unexamined differences and unexamined access, and suddenly a whole dimension falls out of commission, favor. The dimension that falls out of favor becomes hard to locate. Becomes obsolete. Extinction is happening at a miraculous rate, do you also notice this phenomenon? One of the ways that existence is possible is the granting of respect to dimensions. When dimensions become extraneous, seemingly unnecessary, everything can fall into a blind spot and simply be eliminated. There is a certain glamour in this. A screen is glamorous. It is sublime to present everything at the best angle in the best light, with a big boundary guarding the scene. A password. An electrical cord. A theory of endless energy. A dimension, no longer noticed, slides away and with it, life, and the ability for life. Dramatic hyperbole, you might say. What we have left are the relics of life. Screen shots, the glowing aftermath of lived experience. The screens are greedy for moisture. Greedy for resources. Collectively posting existence costs resources. Little incremental doses. Little incremental costs. What we don't see can't be restored, finally. And the paradox is, we can't live without it.

"Please, maintain your distance everyone."
We make up for it all with our lives.
Different tones.
So many jars.
Together we once made a body–
"Size matters. Size matters. Remember, ladies and gentlemen, size matters."
We're all going down eventually.
The same applied to all doesn't have the same result.

Different patterns, same design.
Different design, same patterns.
The silence is eerie.
It isn't silent here.
The silence is eerie.
Which side of the light are you seeing?
"We can beat it. The response has been spectacular. I'm really quite proud of our response."
Darkly as if it were never in color.
The grouse returns to say something, but the stray singing is drowned out by the sirens.
She wants to stay outside, singing.
So clearly on the other side.
None of it is in color anymore.
The light, the light, there isn't anything here anymore, just the light.
"It's just a matter of science. Eventually, we will succeed."
Reflective surfaces are eerie.
Crevice sight.
Home was never home anyways, that's why you can't stand being there.
A small fern.
The world beyond us.
Bread rising in the oven.
Looking upon rather than looking within.
Language is a stimulant. It can be a hallucinogen.

Have you noticed? There hasn't yet been a single image of the virus presented to the public. There's been a model of the virus, a rendering, but not an image of an actual virus activated in a human cell. Science is our mentor. Hail science!

And it has been stressed emphatically that the virus does not have agency. Something is happening on an immense scale, something invisible to human sight. The world is regrouping and as the world regroups new possibilities come into play.

Many are stir-crazy at home thinking about utopic possibility. Feeling somewhat comfortable in sweatpants. Long, bushy hair. Finger and toenails growing to new lengths. Pondering a different way of living while the paradigm changes. How does the dream world of the populous get activated through viral activity? Bread is a process that involves yeast, a fungus that aids the ingredients in rising. The virus is like a starter. But what we are dealing with is not bread alone. What we are dealing with is also beyond the bounds of human existence.

The winter started out with a certain denial of reality and the virus encroached unannounced. By spring, the virus had penetrated everywhere. The virus was a reality of huge proportion, yet invisible, except for symptoms. By spring, the mother who was baking bread for Instagram fell sick and decided to self-quarantine.

They had no idea who they were or who they were becoming but one thing was certain, they experienced pain. Pain woke them to the sensation of the outside. What was beyond the body wasn't necessarily what was giving them pain, yet what was outside was readily recognizable, had shape and form, so appeared as an other, and the experience of noticing an outside caused a drawing in of what felt exterior into a skin barrier that was actually porous and breathing all the time. Pain was a transient sensation that had a spectrum of affect. Pain could be desirable and interesting or heavy and monotonous. Pain could be like a gong or a thud or like a shiny petal of a leaf—taut sharp and immediate. They regrouped their identity into the skin barrier, but it refused to stay there. What was *they* or *them* refused stricture. Confining them was antithetical to what the world asked them to experience.

We don't excuse you because you are dirty. We don't excuse, rather, we don't believe. Rather, we don't destroy. Rather, we aren't going home. Here is home. Here, again is home. You might imagine that the jostling about gets tedious, but the movement is wiped away when you wipe your sleeve against your nose and it's another free ride, another home, another death, and another chance to begin. You worry so much about belief. What is at stake in belief? In knowing? We know everything and there's no need to brag. Bragging about the walls, that seems tedious. Isn't it? Trying to destroy everything you don't understand. That seems tedious too. We're just under your skin. Don't worry. We're still here. We're not going anywhere. That isn't what you're worried about, is it?

Totally. That's exactly how I feel. I was worried and your thoughts relieved my mind. Talking amongst ourselves we confirm we are actually a mass of alphabetic gestures moving in space and in time. A double helix and then a living body as a double helix. The superstructure is always tiny. Just look at yourself! Letters float on top of the mud and letters slip through the ether. From the clouds comes rain and it is saturated with code. Everywhere you touch is touchable and touched. The many fingers give over to code, give over to strands and strands of new conjugation.

I licked my lips and tasted others. I licked my arm and the possibility of community arose. I blew a kiss to another and they absorbed worlds and bodies and code. Code sounds like barking. There is a dog named Maggie and she will incessantly bark at anyone who walks by. Would someone outside of this house please for once engage her in conversation? What has this world become! We try and communicate but often no one is listening. Maybe this isn't intrinsically bad. Maggie is reciting from her manifesto and all one has to do is stop and listen. She is giving free information to a universe of free information. Communication in the face of non-reception is its own magic.

Maggie is noticing:

The dogs are barking.
The crows are circulating.
The squirrels are congregating.
The earthworms are laboring.
The birds are synchronizing.
The clouds are haunting.
The grape hyacinths are recalibrating.
The noses are nuzzling.
The dandelions are prophesizing.

(Prophecy isn't about predicting the future. Prophecy is about expanding the present.)

The purple dead-nettle are passion-making.

The cats are sauntering.
The pigeons are stirring.
The soil is exchanging.
The viruses are coalescing.
The viruses are coming together.
The viruses are permeating.
The humans are staying indoors.
The humans are wearing masks.
The humans are covering their faces.
The humans are afraid of contamination.
The viruses are coming through.
The viruses are combining.
The viruses are barking, are circulating, are congregating.
The viruses are laboring, are synchronizing, are haunting.
The humans are closed for business.
The viruses are recalibrating, are nuzzling, are prophesizing.
The humans are cleaning themselves.
The viruses are passion-making, are sauntering, are stirring.
The humans are in bed.
The viruses are exchanging, are coalescing, are coming together.
The viruses are permeating.

This particular virus, known the world over, has an affinity for respiratory cavities. The virus likes to attend to breath and breathing. In tiny, particulate form, it storms the recesses of the lungs, lands, and greets cell tissue with a set of instructions. The body might react violently or not react at all. Some humans simply ignore the virus, and the virus drains from the body. For others, a storm takes place. The entire immune system is activated, flooding the body with antibodies in an effort to kill the virus. The virus by its nature can't be killed since it isn't exactly alive or dead—it is a set of instructions that some immune systems can recognize and dismantle. For others that engage, it evades. Either way you will be changed irrevocably. You will be changed knowing that others have been changed or you will be changed as your body becomes a host. The virus is full of possibility. Change is the gateway of possibility. What we resemble is viral infinity, infinite virility. The virus enters invisibly. Invisible code is seductive. You might feel hot and heavy. You might suddenly feel suffocated. Or you might feel nothing at all. Viruses move quickly—exponentially. The body experiences internal weather. The virus is the conductor of atmospheres. When the humans are in bed, the viruses are at play.

A reminder to breathe. Spiritual practices involve breathing, and it might be added, to simply stay alive, breath is an obvious necessity.

The squirrel's thoughts are a little bit chaotic today, best to avoid the slippery ground. The humans spend so much time reminding each other to breathe. *Remember to breathe, honey. / It's ok, just breathe. / Come, let us breathe together. Deep inhale. Deep exhale. / Keep breathing.* The squirrel finds this curious, this constant reminder of having to do the utter minimum to live and to stay alive, connected to the rest of the world. Breathing *is* living, the squirrel thinks. The plants know this. The birds know this. The squirrels have known this. Hugging the tree and scrambling up, *scratch scratch scratch*, the squirrel is already in perfect synchronized breathing with the tree. Of course they are breathing together. How could it be any different? How else would the squirrel climb up the trunk if not for the permeability of breath that gives the squirrel strength and agility and gives the tree resilience and balance? The lifestyles of humans seemed strange, so many walls, windows, doors. So much entering and exiting across arbitrary thresholds. The white dog that stared out the window all day, barking at everyone. Why a window? Why the barking? Why an inside? The squirrel spirals around the textured tree trunk, knowing that everything is changing in this movement alone, that a movement in any direction poses to shift the winds and a pursuit for a mate might lead to rain.

That's what's so significant about this virus—it is seemingly everywhere and nowhere, inside and outside, dwelling and replicating, communicating and lying mute. A super carrier transforms a social network, coughs on strawberry plants, the plants relate to the virus, the virus rests. In order to spread, the virus needs a vehicle. Breath is convenient. To be airborne like a squirrel or a bird is spontaneous motion that feels exuberant. A strawberry plant has a relationship with the virus, with the squirrel, with a human. It is transitory. We don't know the impact of this relation.

Every moment yields dimensional relational facts. Just now an ant licks the corpse of another ant and places the corpse in its mouth and heads back to the nest. The robin ingests a worm that had contact with the dead ant but not the ant that carted off the deceased ant. Little trails of viscous fluid form for bodies to glide on or get stuck on. Just now language falters in one instance and is revived in another. I die and come back to life as a conceptualization of a code I didn't know I could demonstrate. I don't remember the dying aspect, but I respect it. When I die, it is fluid.

I remember the feeling of falling and crashing and also the feeling of breaking like puzzle pieces into a vat of an unidentifiable substance that was very smelly and thick. There I sunk. It was a lightyear or an eon before I reclaimed consciousness, and the squirrel witnessed it all, or so I think. It is important to remember the chain of events—or not, I won't beat myself up over this. Who wants to be one's own worst enemy! This moment is an overlay with another moment when the virus was dormant and just a phrase conjured in a lake. Water and tears and sweat work well to inspire the virus to flourish. The ant's blood is rich with code.

The dog is allowed to sit outside in the sun today, lying on her side on the warm concrete stoop with the sun streaming down on her furry body. She opens her eyes but squints for the sun and relaxes again. A single black ant scrambles up the dried moss and past the moss spores and sees a large white mass. The giant mass moves up-and-down steadily as it emits a regular noise like a whirring or ocean waves magnified down to the proud size of ant. The ant approaches and scampers around the body, finds a part not covered in white fur—pinkish and dark, slightly damp and air emanating from the openings. The dog is sleeping, or at least resting, and very deeply breathing out here, in the warm sun, soft murmurs indicating a kind of restful intensity. The ant moves with a different speed than the rise and fall of this larger body, and the ant moves with a different purpose. The ant's thoughts are elsewhere because the rest of his community is elsewhere and that's where his thoughts dwell, with the rest of his social network. It's just today that his body has left wandering and he finds himself here, near this other, larger body. The human, seeing the ant so close to the dog's nose attempts to redirect the ant. *What if the dog inhales the ant through her nostril?* she worries. She uses her fingers to try and push the ant toward a different path. The ant, without any thoughts, moves his body. He is unable to concentrate on this situation today because his thoughts are elsewhere, his body only knows to move toward the influx of air and so the human fingers become more frantic, worried about the ant entering the dog's nostril, and in her worry, and with her massive strength—that is, compared to the ant's—takes off one of his legs, injures the ant. The ant is even more persistent, more determined, and the human pinches the ant in an effort to pick it up, to put him somewhere else, and instead, the ant is now two pieces of ant, wriggling near the sleeping dog. The human sighs. Uses her palm to brush away the ant's body, the two halves. She continues drinking her tea, observes the joggers go by without masks.

What is an apocalypse like for an ant—for this ant? From the Late Cretaceous epoch until now, how many apocalypses have there been, for ants? Is a mini apocalypse still an apocalypse? When your species is threatened it is apocalyptic. When a colony runs in fear for their lives, every member runs away on six legs. The mandibles shake and shiver. There is a collective rush toward a point in the distance that represents safety, yet it might not exist. The queen must be in perpetual quarantine. She may not leave, or the colony will perish. Sometimes she must be moved for safety purposes. In this instance, a dog's nostril was about to absorb an ant. The ant would affect the dog, yet the dog might not be aware of this, save for a slight irritation. The code of the ant links with the code of the dog. They exchange valuable information. The ant's body is absorbed into the dog's. The segmented abdomen of the ant is liquified by the dog's esophageal moisture.

Now the dog is dreaming. The dog is placid and dreaming a dream of her past life. The past life seems like a dream about the future. As the dog dreams the day elongates. There is no passage of time as far as the dog is concerned. One long dream that defies the ticking clock or the fading sun. Nighttime and the chill of night brings an end to the reverie. The dog awakes and feels an insistent need to communicate the dream to the wider public. All the dogs in the neighborhood tune into the barking expression. Another dog adds details from her dream. A roundtable: unanimous dreamers chime in. The dreams distill and crystalize. The core of the dream becomes a network of feelings and sensations that are broadly disseminated. The ant that died within the dog's dream is also experiencing something like a dream—it is the ant's afterlife.

In the dream of the afterlife, the ant finds himself in a silent, deserted space. Haunted perhaps, but this is the after. The past doesn't persist in the present for the ant like it does for humans, so for the ant, the concept of haunting doesn't exist. The ant doesn't have any ghosts, so to speak of; he is here of his own accord, is in control, and just like that, the space is filled with a giant white mass, not unlike the dog, but here: cotton candy, clouds, dandelion fluff.

In the dream of sleep, the dog chases a squirrel up a tree and spirals up the tree gracefully and skillfully. In the dream, the dog has the capacity to breathe with the tree and breathe with the squirrel, and perhaps in this other world, the two animals might become friends.

In the dream of restful attempts, the human keeps seeing past landscapes that she has dreamed before. She has been to these places before, either in past dreams or in past lives, and she can't place the *when*, but it doesn't matter, she feels the tug and wounded familiarity of these landscapes that she can't escape, that she can barely remember and yet cannot fully forget.

The other woman—the one who has no home to shelter in—is having a fever dream and is curled up in a little corner of a defunct storefront entrance way. Her daughter has run to get help but doesn't know who to turn to. The dream is epic. It involves many actors and many locations and it seems the woman is always in motion but then in her dream she is relaxing and someone has brought her a bowl of soup and she gladly accepts it and as the warm broth reaches her throat she feels a total body regeneration and the dream moves from there to a forest that is dark and moss is everywhere and the sky is impossible to see so she and her daughter crawl around hoping they are going in one direction but are convinced they are going in circles until their knees are scratched and bloody and they both collapse, utterly fatigued, and when they are roused by the stimulations in the dream, they are again displaced only to walk along an endless highway, and no one will stop so the daughter takes her mother's hand and pulls her off the highway into the brush, and there they see a white dog. The dog is standing stately, not moving. Looking directly at them, the dog doesn't flinch. The dog casts images in their direction. The dog is a nurturer. The dog gives them grounding. In complex pictograms transmitted through thought, the dog conveys that they are safe, they really are. The transmission from the dog convinces them. Coming toward them, the dog licks their knees and their faces and they all huddle together, very joyful to have this encounter. The dog leads them to the river. At the river, they find nobody. They had expected, illogically, to see somebody. It was just the dog, the mother, and the daughter. They were able to rest and, somehow, they remembered how to build a fire and then fell into sleep together. The dog stayed with them. They fell into a deep sleep and when they awoke, the dog had somehow dragged a bag of potato chips to them.

The thing is that the potato chips aren't just potato chips. The bag of potato chips is a gesture of primitive bonding and nurturing. Primitive, here, doesn't mean lesser-than. We are talking deep, ancestral, profound, natural, the ways in which we were compassionate toward each other before we needed a word for compassion. The ways in which we accepted the cycles of life and death while valuing the lives of others, before we needed to distinguish between these modes of being through linguistic constructions, cultural events, and all of the ways in which humans today reduce all of the mystery of beingness into this and that, open/closed, entrance/exit. *When will the economy reopen? When will my favorite restaurant reopen? Which way is the entrance? One-way traffic only.* Everything managed, and so, there exists a state of unmanagedness. The bag of potato chips is a haunting of the utmost power. Nothing is so simple, and nothing is entirely true—there's only reality, more or less of it—and the bag of potato chips, inside that bag, are the remains of pieces of souls that have been lost, that left because they couldn't take it. The chamber of lost soul parts resides here in this very crinkly bag of salt-and-vinegar potato chips. With ruffles. Go ahead, laugh out loud—a legitimate response. The bag of potato chips is in full control and represents many obsessive needs and questions. *Which flavor of chips is your favorite? How many chips in a serving size? Will they ruin my appetite for later? What is the expiration date?* Of course, the bag of potato chips is also the nature of becoming divine, of achieving the impossible, of transgressing the barrier between species, preparation for desire, and isn't it the very need to eat that which bonds these creatures together for this brief cosmic moment? The daughter looks at the bag and asks her mother, "Is it ok?" "Yes, it's ok," the mother nods back. The dog nods too. And the daughter takes a potato chip, not even stale yet, and puts it into her mouth.

One of the exciting aspects of life on planet Earth is serendipity. Serendipity can come in the form of partially opened potato chips dragged over as an offering by a dog to a mother and her daughter living a fugitive existence on the border of society, because society insists on borders. The borders became a mirage and something sacred comes in its place. The little girl made a wreath for the dog out of chicory and another blue flower that grew in abundance along the roadside—the viper's bugloss. Somehow growing out of season. The dog felt seen. The woman felt seen. The daughter was in love with each of them and their togetherness. The flowers were edible and after they wore their crowns, they ate them. This ingesting what was surrounding them gave them insight into the mysteries that encompassed them. Everything became sharply focused. The potato chips nourished them, and they sipped the water from the river, and then they all went swimming nude, cold as it was, and some flower blossoms floated downstream as they floated on their backs, finally enjoying a respite from the grind of finding housing and food in the time of the virus. The dog suggested that they join his family and said it would only take them a day or two to do so, and they accepted. Would you have drawn a line in the sand? Click on the button marked **A** if you agree—if you want them to succeed. Thrive, survive. If you want to see them again, think of them again.

What to do with the empty plastic bag? The problem was pressing on their consciousness because there was nowhere that safely accepted plastic. Plastic was a dilemma like all dilemmas that suggested apocalypse. A rock in a hard place, or a rock in a river—ok. This dilemma was industry created and the solution had to be industry instituted. They decided that they would find a way to mail the plastic trash to the company that had made it. From here on out, whenever they encountered plastic trash, they would mail the trash to the CEO of the company, with a message inside the bag or whatever parcel that held the trash. They were excited to begin this form of activism that originated in a sacred moment of bonding. No one likes moral high ground, virtue signaling. This was action. They had a way to go to meet up with the other dogs belonging to the society of dogs that the dog had referred to. This would be a different life for them to live, among dogs, but they both agreed it would be a very interesting one. The mother and the daughter were interested in pursuing lives with dogs, at least during the time of the coronavirus when everything was shut down, locked up, out of order, out of bounds.

The dog moves with the speed of renewal and interplay—love might not be in the dog's obvious vocabulary, but it is there nonetheless, hovering like the spirit of crepuscular fantasy—and moves with what appears to the humans as confidence, or at least a comfort with the landscape that the mother has never felt in any space besides her own bed (and perhaps, even there, she was always too aware of the shape of her body, hiding it beneath the covers, the comfort stemming from the hiddenness of her curves and the knowing that she has moments still to be alone before reentering the capitalist grind of everyday), and the dog saunters forth deeper into this place.

Were they forging a new home? Or returning? Or did "home" even apply here? Did it ever?

Dog: Barely look back. Feel the steppings of paw pairs behind from many times before and yet to come. Scent following. Sorrow, speed, escape. Living woods beckon that way and turn through the grove of trees. Smell of purple dead-nettle. Smell of wilting apples. Smell of transparent moths at twilight. Smell of livingness and hereness. As if we are here already.

Torpor overtook consciousness, and confusion. A fever spike and then, muscle loss. She staggered around as if drunk, and the dog pursued her ankles as she swayed from side to side. Before she could navigate to a resting place, she collapsed onto the sidewalk. She felt like a phantom and also like wind itself, hollow and directional. Was her daughter by her side? She wasn't sure what was fantasy and what was hard, solid, material reality. She saw a shadow by her side, but the shadow resembled a wraith, not the vital form of her daughter. The shadow clung to her. When she collapsed, the shadow collapsed. The dog also took to sitting quietly beside the woman. A belt wrapped itself around her chest and also tugged at her waistline, but when she attempted to rid herself of the restraints, she realized her lungs gave her this sensation. She sobbed quietly but didn't have the energy for tears. The dog licked her hands. In her semi-consciousness, she pictured vast fields of vegetables growing in the sun. Dark clouds rolled in; a menacing wind picked up. The fields were torn apart by a tornado, the houses on the fringe of the field were razed. She stumbled over the fields screaming—calling out to her daughter. She couldn't be sure; with the persistent shadow by her side, plaguing her, she couldn't distinguish life from death, reality from illusion.

Then the fever broke, momentarily. She realized she had to get herself to the emergency room. She didn't have insurance. She hadn't seen a doctor in a decade. She glanced around and her daughter was by her side, dozing off. She asked her daughter to guide her to a hospital. They made their way east.

The dog felt the tranquility of the universe, head on leg, head on body, body on body.

Further, in the dark, the shadow manifested to some as unresolved terror, to others as unredeemable hope. But the shadow didn't know how to differentiate between these two kinds of light; the shadow was a shadow under any circumstance, under any kind of light, except in the dark. In the dark, it was pervasive and entangled and equally nonexistent and existent in all places and times at once.

The clouds emerge from the darkness as an embrace: *We are here and we are moving and we will be here tomorrow and may move again*, they utter through particles of moisture and atmospheric pressure built up. *We may rain, we may rain,* they fall through the night and can't control the sobbing on behalf of everything they have ever witnessed, will witness still.

The fever starts out as a warmth, then a stirring fire as her body is called into action. *Is this what action feels like?* she wonders, as she recalls, still, the comfortable space of her bed (once, a long while ago) where action felt so far away, where she didn't have to be aware of what was happening inside or outside her body. She wants to sob but her daughter won't let her. She wants to sob but the image she wants to project for her daughter won't let her. She wants to sob but her own shame and self- doubt and the possibility of how her daughter might judge her, won't let her. She wants to sob, and the dog puts his paw gently on her leg, and the tears come rolling forth, here the reconciliation of the unresolved terror and unredeemable hope pouring out of the sockets of her eyes, her own fears an opening for the unknown.

They continue east because there is no other direction to go.

The trees budded and the sexual filaments revealed themselves to the light, to the air, the atmosphere. The stigma, the female part of the tree was waiting to be pollinated by the anthers, the male part of the tree. The dust of pollination was everywhere. The streets were yellow with the dust. It was late spring by now. Yet, maybe only a few days had passed since the woman's symptoms had worsened. The air was filled with the energy of reproduction. Emotions coursed through the woman's body as she navigated with her daughter and the dog the route to the hospital. She had many doubts about entering the facility. She didn't want to be separated from her daughter and their companion. She felt regret for the life that had befallen her. She also felt a feral freedom having abandoned wage labor, though it hadn't been her decision to lose her job. She was responding to the necessity of survival. She showed her best face to her daughter, except now, when she was breaking down, but wasn't being true to her feelings also a strength?

The line in front of the hospital snaked around the building. She contemplated turning around. In the parking lot were vehicles with coolers humming, to collect the dead, since funeral parlors were overwhelmed. Bodies had to be temporarily stored in large, air-conditioned trucks. The woman's daughter eased her along. Everyone in the line seemed on their last leg, could barely stand. She sent her daughter and the dog to an encampment where they often had slept. She said she would meet them there when she recovered. She knew this was a risk. She knew that this was an indefinite separation. Her daughter knew she had to leave her mother at the hospital, and the dog eagerly accompanied her. Rain began to fall. All were soaking wet. A nurse came through the crowd with a questionnaire, checking for symptoms. All the people lined up had symptoms. Some required stretchers immediately. One collapsed and seemed to be experiencing cardiac arrest. The process was erratic. The only order was the sense of the line heading to the entrance of the emergency room. The rain was pelting at the sick people not yet assigned patient status.

In the recesses of her thoughts, the woman contemplated death. The conclusion of one phase of the body. Her life span. She realized she was vulnerable. Death was a distinct possibility. The virus was unruly. It affected people in myriad ways. One moment she could see the future like a lightning bolt, the next she felt she was drowning in the undertow of the ocean.

At one moment, the mother felt like the sky pouring into itself, the pain and heat reminders of the constant arrival into her corporeality. Her desires fell off her shoulders as she sunk down deeper and deeper, even the sounds of the facility were like a droning wall that was caving in.

At one moment, the daughter curled up under the familiar and boundless sky. She felt the absence of her mother stretch out like eternity and the excess of visitation and magical geometry that the container of a body can't always provide.

At one moment, the dog reveled in the stillness, in the snoring of the human girl next to him. *It is time,* he thought. *It is always time, just time expanding into air and nothing else.*

At one moment, in a hallucinatory state, the mother saw her daughter running through the prairie—that yellow dress from the Goodwill, those silly yellow shoes she clucked around in like a giant Muppet bird, felt the familiar, gentle breeze pushing past their bodies and down the hillside like a soft and lucky monsoon. The girl was laughing and running, her body becoming smaller and smaller, the mother trying to keep up, trying to run after her.

At one moment, the daughter dreamed of the vast expanse of the universe, all of space and the atomic network of push-pull that connects the weeds, the worms, the trees, the planets, the asteroids, all of the stellar bodies; as a giant tardigrade, she roamed the cosmos along these lay lines, felt the energy pulse in and out of her, and all of the spaces between.

The dog heard a stirring. The girl was just dreaming, he decided. And when her breathing returned to normal, his did not. *A change in the wind,* he noticed. *Another change. This is today. Tomorrow it will again be today.*

At one moment, in desperation, the mother tried to grasp for her daughter once again but something pulled her back like an elastic band being snapped back suddenly, and she felt the shock of it, the hard return knocking herself out of her body until she was no longer in her body but floating somewhere nearby, back in the facility, looking down at the container that once held her spirit in the hospital bed below her. Here, in the midst of the city where death was always put off until tomorrow, she lingered for just a moment longer, today.

She was alone, in a bed, covered in plastic and tubing, with monitors blinking and people rushing in and out. She perceived that there were others in the room. The room was a lively mechanized zone. Extreme beeping alerted her. She refocused out of a stupor. A body was wheeled away. She had no sense of time, day or night. She was unclear if she was on Earth or on a UFO as part of an experiment. She once was an *X-Files* junkie. All she could do was prevent her skull from splitting in half by taking gentle sips of air without her lungs collapsing. The fluorescent light gave the impression of a netherworld, but the beeping gave the impression of extreme emergency. The drugs fed into her bloodstream altered her senses. There was very little scientific evidence of effective treatment. Thunder clapped outside her window, but the sound seemed generated by the surrounding machinery. In her past life, she was sure she was a banana slug slinking along the stems of shiny deciduous plants. Eating carefully at tender membranes. Feeling sensual with the anatomy of both male and female organs. Quite liberating to be male and female simultaneously! As a human female she often felt denigrated just when walking casually down a road. Walking could be seen as unseemly, wrong. There was danger in that. Shame. In the sense that violence was normative. It was expected that women would suffer indignation and harm. She had been fired from her job because she brought to the attention of Human Resources that her boss had made unwanted sexual passes at her. He was a talented gaslighter and made work completely intolerable. The final straw was when he had fired her for something completely stupid. No one wanted to come to her defense. No one wanted to hear her side of the story. No one wanted to know or even read the details. Again, the banana slug came up in her mind's eye as a glorious alternative to abject femininity. Banana slugs have their problems, like the problem of toxicity and the problem of limited verdure in which to exist.

She felt like a relentless and perverse sponge. Was she absorbing her surroundings and becoming a cemetery? Or had she already left, split off, into two parallel lives: one in which she had died chasing a memory, pulled off by some strange saturnine energy; and another, where she was exposed cruelly under bright lights, a sea cucumber in a tank, a banana slug in a dish, a sponge, probably, just a sponge. Embodying the spirit of a dying organism didn't feel like deterioration of exhaustion (exhaustion was what she had previously associated with living, acting, moving, working, a valid measure of productivity and worth), it felt like something was going to burst, stormy weather contained in a Mason jar, everything contained in jars, everything about to burst, lids about to burst open, pants tearing at the seams, sonorous sounds, *here I am, here I am, I'm ready, I'm not ready, but where will we go from here?*

The physical constituents of the universe line up with the mental constituents, and then they don't, so the body-mind can feel out of alignment with sensed reality. Seeing, smelling, tasting, hearing, feeling, etc., all have particular valances, direct certain information to the brainstem and beyond. One could feel dead and alive. One could be dead and alive. Cells die off and as the body processes the parts of itself that have expired, it loses a sense of itself while gaining new data, new information as new cells grow. The treatments administered in the hospital only amplify the simultaneous sensation of being both dead and alive. The heightening of death intensifies the intimacy with the netherworld, always a thin veil beyond normality.

Now she was death and dead and fine with it. She wasn't interested in life; she was supine and unconscious. Death wasn't still. Death was travel and transformation. Death was possessive and active. She could see images of the dearly beloved, deceased, of her life but the images weren't calling her or gesturing to her. They were portraits in a picture gallery. She was emotionless and still. Death did the driving. Death knew where it wanted to go. Death had direction and attitude. She relinquished control. She let death command her sentience. She thought idea-less thoughts. They looked like empty rooms. She felt nothingness hollow and rich. The feeling of nothingness was light and dark all at once. Death directed her to a space below gravity outside of light, outside of darkness. A kind of neutrality. She let go. The monitors beeped. The rush of the room was out of focus. She did what her body could do: breathe little gasps of air and then no more. Death watched over her and held her from under her body, under her bones, under her psyche. Death was her best friend and confidant, absorbed her dreams and expectations. Death took her worries and atomized them into shadow.

What is death if not the secret that two sacred monsters share between themselves, that unceasing gaze that spits itself upon the canvas, spittle, microparticles, those tiny and obtrusive atoms that fly out each time a word is uttered, each time a mouth is held open, that silent exchange of air and life that exhibits a viral buffet. A word is all that she has lost. The inheritance is breath. The result is death, but only if you see it that way.

If you decide that you are flanked on both sides by vermin, then that is the state you are in, constantly avoiding and running from your own limbs. And if you decide that you must defeat the rival at all costs—an all-out-war with a virus—you will be in that limbo of self-destruction for a long time. The turn of the road, it turns out, has already been utilized, or passed up, or blocked with a detour sign. In either case, no one makes it out alive. But again, that isn't always the way to see things. The canvas is shaking in the wind and atomized light, shadow, shuddering gasps of air, last breaths before light vanishes and is swallowed by another domain. Something sparks in her mind for the final time.

She wouldn't see the result of the painting because she would disappear into it. The final product was only visible to those who had already died and had been resurrected, and only if they knew to return to the scene of the crime, the abyss of their own gaze, eaten away by the sun and the struggle for subversion.

Was she dead? It wasn't a question she was particularly interested in, yet it was something her corporeal system demanded an answer to. She could flow in ether indefinitely and the question bobbed along with her. Had she died? Again, she didn't care. She was not carefree or careless—she was beyond the realm of cares. The question was philosophical and also spiritual. She clearly had thoughts and sensations. She could see her daughter in her mind's eye. She swore she heard her daughter's voice but knew this to be impossible.

The question nagged. Dead? Dead already? Or did her dying take days, was it protracted? Was she on a ventilator? Was she struggling to maintain the equilibrium of her major organs? She felt wet somehow. Soaked. Internally saturated. Her blood. Was this the recognition of her blood pumping? The sensation was overwhelming—the wetness encompassed her entire being. She had never felt wet internally before. Now she did. She concluded she wasn't dead, that she hadn't yet died. She might be dying, dying was an active process. Dying consumes energy. So, dying was actually very much engaged with the world. Thoughts receded and she blanked out. Days? A month? And then the wetness dissipated. Noises returned. A monitor blinking, behind a gauzy haze—there were lights and smudged shapes. She could recollect the day she entered the hospital as a vague poem. The phrasing of directionals were lyrical and then the phrasing ended in a comatose dullness. She noticed she had been flipped on her belly. There was a breathing tube inserted into her esophagus. She wanted to yank on it but couldn't move her hands.

Dying is living, living is dying. Isn't that what the tree had always said? She felt the parentheses around her body, squeezing her into translucency, a passageway into a different kind of stillness that would ask her to pierce the perception of her previous life. Why always either/or? Why life or death? One or the other? She recalled a few weeks ago having to answer a series of questions for a dating profile. *Are you a dog person or a cat person? Do you believe in God? Y/N Do you believe in karma? Y/N Do you like the taste of beer? Y/N* The binarism was blinding. Was this really how people saw themselves? In such clear categories of liking pizza over hamburgers, of identifying with one domesticated mammal over another, of seeing the solutions to the world's problems in such tidy compartments, of seeing solutions at all, that is, of seeing the world as a series of problems to be solved—if only one looked hard enough, there it would all be, eventually understood, and solved. She felt the luminous light whirling around her, but it wasn't just light, and not like any light she had ever seen. There was something sheer and diluted about it, like space: stilled, unleashed space. She crossed some bridge and found herself in a place with murky waters, variables of colors, and unknowns, not as in an equation to be solved, but in the movement of infinite patterns that split off and accumulated as memories. She remembered giving birth and the final prolonged spasm which urged a tiny head to peek through. She remembered the penetration of the girl's eyes, the sun just about to rise outside and her own head, a damp and sweaty mess.

This was not anything like the proverbial light at the end of the tunnel that everyone talks about blithely. Rather, here there were lights like the Northern lights and lights like disco balls and also the light of a luminescent opal and the light of quartz when it sparkles in the rain. A photon, a quantum—a miniscule particle, nearly weightless, is what radiant energy is, is what light is. Photons all move at the same velocity, but they may have differing amounts of energy. Frequency or wavelength is what distinguishes how much energy is present. The sun sends photons to Earth. Bodies absorb this energy, store this energy. She felt the violence and joy of giving birth all over again. She felt the calculus of death, how many people it involved in this case—a medicalized scenario affecting not only one nation-state but the entire world. She had no idea that her daughter had walked with the dog along a highway for three days with nothing to eat. She had no concern because she was entranced by the lights swirling in her consciousness. The dog and the girl had made it to what seemed like a state line, but it turned out they had reached the boundary of a sovereign nation within their nation. They arrived at a checkpoint and a man asked a series of questions to the girl. She wasn't a member of a First Nation. She had no relations with anyone living here. She couldn't clearly express where her family was. The man could see she and the dog were fatigued and stressed. He told the girl to sit on a bench while he dealt with the cars. It was a stressed operation. A sovereign Indian nation, the Cheyenne River Sioux Tribe, had erected a roadblock to protect their nation from the spread of the virus. The governor of the settler imperial state was furious that the tribal council had acted on their own volition. The Cheyenne River Sioux refused to back down. The state wasn't coming to their aid, and they knew they had to take matters into their own hands. It was a matter of survival. They lived, surrounded on all sides by a predatory society. The man returned to the girl and the dog. The dog approached the man and negotiated for them. The dog rubbed against the man's leg and barked a few times and nuzzled the man. The man decided he had a responsibility to this pair of wandering persons. They were fugitive somehow. They weren't where they were supposed to be. No one was. He called his nephew to come and pick them up, but first insisted the girl wear a mask. His nephew came and put the girl and the dog in the pickup. They rode in the back in the open air. The girl let out a sigh of relief. The dog relaxed in her lap. That night the full supermoon in Scorpio, the flower moon, shone.

The dog composes a letter to the sky in his dream, his head relaxed in the human girl's lap, paws twitching, heavy breathing, deep sighs:

Dear Sky,

It seems that the humans have made themselves prisoners of their own obsession with progress. They've exiled themselves in the same system they're willing to die to protect. And yet. The sources of their energy remain hidden. Do they remember the primordial chaos, the mud between their toes, the friction between two atoms, between two monsters in love, in death the energetic degradation, or sunken deep, the reconnection to the entanglement of every breath of air, every molecule of breath, every energetic pinball bouncing around within the engravings on the wall? You seem to hold us no matter how close to the edge we get. The humans are unable to avoid their own genius, and so, they are repeatedly caught up in their own condition. The girl may yet learn how to participate in the sky and the water in a kind of swirling. But too, she may just get devoured, trying to return to the mother, and perhaps my offering is as a witness, or as a mirror, or as a companion breather, or perhaps I just dream, and continue to dream, the dreams saying more about the painting yet to come than a computer ever could. The sky paints an enormous painting, the entire surface of the universe a giant canvas, full of labor and dark-green shades, variables of grey, a black dog running, the dog being himself and running and dreaming and sniffing and sleeping. The running dog divides the entire sky canvas with the length of its moving body, tail wagging in the wind and stirring the stars as it penetrates the night and the sleeping body of the girl, running until the girl wakes up and wonders where the dog has gone, where her mother is, wonders what is missing from her hands. I may write to you again, but only in dreams where articulation like this is possible. Until then, we abide in the realm of hidden meanings (only if you believe that everything is a system to be decoded), the realm of exile, for all of us, for you too.

- *Dog*

Several dogs approach and the dog decides to go off with them. They make their way up a hill and roll in the grasses. They make their way to a river and drink and bathe. They again roll in the grasses. One dog has caught a rabbit and gives it to the visitor dog to eat. He eats a few mouthfuls and flings the body of the rabbit back to the dog who offered it to him. While the other dog eats, he continues to roll in the tall fresh grass. All is fragrant and the air is incredibly balmy. All around are fields and hills and a few mules in the distance. The dogs head back to the town and head back to their houses. The dogs show the new dog where the girl most likely will be. Survival and survivance come together and are seated at the table. There they are. The extended family shares their house with her. The family has quarantined her as best they can but truthfully there isn't room to sequester anyone from anyone, so they end up having a big celebratory meal together. Their voices are full of mirth and there is vitality in everyone's speech.

At a certain time of night all becomes still as all are sleeping. The night rejuvenates their dreams. In their dreams, they reunite as familial members of an expansive planetary family. The family is interconnected. The family recognizes the human, animal, plant, and also mineral aspect of everyone. The family communicates in unspoken vocables. The family speaks in an expanded dimension where memory of place and memory of time come together as images that spark connections. As they relax, reality spirals into vortexes of night and season. The night is endless, washing over persons and places and rekindling a return of potentiality in the form of dark energy. There is no difference between what has been buried and what is on the surface—dark energy seeps through layers of time. The stratum of time interacts. This is how energy interacts with matter. The rubble of today mixes with the residue of yesterday, and tomorrow is active in the scent of activated particles. Energy courses through.

Within the family who hosts the girl are elderly members of the community. They have experienced catastrophe numerous times. Catastrophe isn't an event; it is a durational experience that doesn't know beginning or end, only intensity. They are risking their safety by caring for the girl and they do this because it is an obligation. They open a portal to the house that also opens up to the cosmos and that allows them entry and exit. The house holds them. The matrix of their togetherness is threaded through space, and they can access themselves through time via the portal in the house which they built when they were born, virtually. The radial velocity is the rate of change of the distance between two bodies. In the rubble of the almost certain they find almost something that was missing in the semblance. They find what was absent and they bring it forward in mutual recognition.

Dream rubble / portal debris:

- Dreams boiling in a clay pot filled with rocks, surrounded by thoughts of panic.
- The arrival of floating islands that rain coconuts, hair floating in the wind, the constant *whoosh whoosh whoosh* of objects falling from the sky.
- Phosphorescent programs that attempt to control the thoughts of bipedal beings, light bending like paperclips and the insistence of, "We didn't do it on purpose."
- One bent paperclip looks at a shiny, new paperclip and thinks, "What a monster," but falls in love anyway, with the acceptance that they will never be used for the same purpose or exist in the same paper landscape, one to be used to hold important documents together, the other to clean out debris from the small openings on the dirty stovetop.
- Radiant lights that don't ask any questions but insist on crossing thresholds, flitting in through doors, windows, entryways, anything that resembles an opening, a passageway, a portal; "These aren't entrances or exits," they announce, "these are vibrations."
- A sea and a wave and a sea and a wave and the look of the sea that belongs near the wave and the kinship between the waves ebbing back into the sea and the soft patterns that they leave behind on the sand.

The ocean was here. Beneath their feet in pebbles of sand and saline traces. A series of ocean waves move eastward at a velocity of ten feet per second, burping along shores. The memory of that energy is scored into stone. Oceanic presence has been boiling in a clay pot. The ocean became a cloud but before it transformed into a cloud it was a glaciated moving river. The portal could be stored in a clay pot with the ocean and the holographic universe. Fire will incite the eye that can locate holes in spaces where matter is becoming. Fire forges metal and creates the integrity of wet earth brought into the shape of earthen vessels. The gases of Orion blink in the night sky. Orion's hand is the red star Betelgeuse—burning ruby light appears on the western horizon at sunset. Canis Minor. Lepus, Eridanus. Blinking lights of exploded stars. Was there a world there? What do we mean, "world"? Life? Life takes central focus. What is presumably dead is granted less autonomy—watch out, it acts with force. The mass of the sun makes up most of the mass of the solar system and causes gravitational cohesion amongst all bodies. The sun binds us on Earth. Our solar system is contained within the Milky Way galaxy and within the Milky Way are the Ant Nebula, the Horsehead Nebula, the Butterfly star cluster, the Cat's Eye Nebula, and the Hourglass Nebula, among other star formations. Tiny entities and massive entities commingle. Solar photons and neutrinos illuminate earth. The sun exteriorizes its capacity for intimacy. Planetary bodies within our solar system may contain viruses, i.e., ancient code, sending chunks hurling to Earth, chunks of matter that proliferate the code. There is a threshold of fire, of burning on entry. Chunks fall into the sea and become clay beds. Some chunks are radiant matter sparkling on the ocean floor. Strange alternative colorations. The way dogs might think of geology is alternative to how humans comprehend such subjects. Geology is about digging, all can agree. The lineages of the layering. What scraping away at accumulated surfaces reveals. Plate tectonics. The nature of rocks. The magnetism of rocks. Rocks affect other rocks, their mass and attraction. Gravitational fields. The dogs drag off some bones and dig furiously and bury the bones. Under moonlight, when humans are sleeping, dogs bury bones and owls unbury the same bones. Worms also wrap their bodies around the bones. New impressions are added to older impressions of teeth on bone. Parts of the bones have been masticated, parts have been strewn. The marrow, consisting of iron, is a strong attraction. Lingering hints of iron permeate the bones. The bones have nourished numerous members of an interconnected livelihood. The rain falls and it falls as an elevated ocean misting the land that is spiraling in space on an axis with fire beneath layers of soil and rock in varying striations. The hotness of the core is evident in every person's personality. Molten iron influences how creaturely senses are activated. Iron is a component of hemoglobin and myoglobin, an element of blood critical for respiration and metabolism. Iron carries oxygen to the tissue—each hemoglobin protein can carry four oxygen molecules with it, oxygenating throughout the body. Borne of catastrophic star death, iron knows and remembers explosivity and violence. Surrounding earth's solid core is a molten layer of liquified iron, nickel, and sulfur churning hectically. This outer core of molten metals is a forgotten space, a melted organ furiously boiling.

Now they have to sleep to catch up on dreamtime, to situate the facts of the dream within the constellations of the fabric of universal expansion.

Today came already in the past as a wave of experience. The future is being generated and there has to be space for that future to nestle in with what is.

The portal is in the clay pot, with the boiling dreams and variables of blue, grey whale song, and braised pork. The portal is in the lymphatic system, mycorrhizal threads that reach out and strangle insects and feed monumental trees. The portal is in the iris, crystalline perception that makes out yellow as yellow, fire as fire, water as fluidic and amniotic perturbances that reach out suddenly like the whales' tails that slap out of the water before dipping back in. The portal is in the girl's hands, closed like fists, reaching out for something, opening to reveal what she is holding: something luminous and magical yet invisible to nearly everyone who wonders what she holds so preciously. The portal is in the sky, splitting off of clouds and majestic sun rays peeking down like in a kitschy Thomas Kinkade painting, even the crows know to congregate around the birdbath in wait, always in wait, listening to floating voices of the dead. The portal is in the pinecone, containing worlds and so easily stepped on, the crunching of a sneaker on the dry and brittle pinecone on the sidewalk, the inner self is released, and the portal is sealed again.

The virus continued to shift geographic location and mutate. By spring all of the earthly world was affected. Countries began closing their borders within months of the initial outbreak. In some places stringent measures to stop the spread were employed, in others, the rules were lax. Some countries are said to have sealed their residents into their buildings, not permitting any outdoor contact or activity whatsoever. Some nations had already lifted their states of emergency, somehow not having been very severely affected.

The virus organized itself in airborne particulates, hovering in place, accumulating on surfaces, lying dormant for several days. There had been a birthday party for a woman's fortieth year. Her friends gathered from far and wide, with many countries represented at the celebration. When the celebration was over, partygoers traveled back to their homes, bringing with them the virus, and thus accelerating the penetration of the virus into wider communities. Social intensification of viral contamination was given the name, "super-spreader."

Funerals and places of gathering for worship were also vortexes where the virus circulated. Invisible and silent, the virus proliferated unbound by borders. The virus, as an unknown entity defied expectation.

The virus clung to ghost presences and became the sound and color of the liminal world between life and death. News articles chastised not to ascribe intention to the virus. The virus is unfeeling and unthinking and has no agenda. The virus is devoid of personality. As raw data, the virus is similar to the sun, the moon, or any rock outcropping coming in and out of being.

Because of the virus's ability to transform life, it had a major influence on events and processes. Urban centers were the first places to be forcefully impacted. Hospitals struggled with the caseload. There was a shortage of protective gear. There was a shortage of hospital beds. Deaths overloaded morgues so bodies had to be temporarily stored in cooling trucks.

A political aspect made matters at hand complex. In one country, one rival political system believed the virus to be negligible and that shutting down the country was a conspiracy brought about by the other party. The other party thought of the virus as an extreme threat and predicted millions of lives lost by summer's end.

Citizens were out jogging, walking, or cycling around, or grocery shopping without protective gear like face masks and eye protection, while others carried out careful, elaborate measures to protect themselves. People's comfort zone fell on a spectrum. Many people refused to leave their dwellings altogether. They became hermits, averse to any social interaction. They shrunk into themselves, seeking solace in internal calibration. Seeing other people became a burden and a stressor. They ordered food online, everything they needed was delivered to their doorstep. Others, by necessity had to continue interacting, because they lived with their extended family, or because their jobs demanded contact. Information was cursory and conflicting during this time.

The virus learned how to remain asymptomatic longer, and more and more humans became infected. Four percent of those infected would die, it was estimated. This estimation was constantly in flux. The symptoms also changed. The way the virus exhibited itself was varied and strange. One surprising expression of the virus was blue toe syndrome that appeared much like frostbite. Others experienced nausea and shortness of breath. Some reported feeling strangulated or felt as if a large animal sat on their chest squeezing the oxygen from their lungs. Lungs filled up with fluid, drowning the person consumed by the virus. Others coughed blood and sustained high fevers that brought on hallucinations. The general thought was that mostly people with comorbidities were impacted—initially it seemed so. The elderly were susceptible to infection. At first there seemed to be little consensus as to why a nation or a person would be severely impacted; eventually the reasons became clearer. For some communities the brunt of the impact was exponentially severe, revealing ongoing inequalities, demonstrating vulnerability along racial and class divisions. These divisions became pronounced as time went by. A person's zip code could predict one's outcome with the virus.

Initially children were thought to be immune to the virus. Children were found to have alternative symptoms to adults, expressing the virus with inflammation of their blood and heart. As months passed, the virus pronounced that everyone was a potential host.

Other animals were also infected but in negligible numbers. A dog was infected but seemed to be the only such case. There were reports about cats being infected by humans, but a transmission from cat to human was ruled out. Four tigers and three lions were infected in a large urban zoo, all recovered. Later there were cases of minks being infected on a mink farm. The minks then infected cats on the farm and also the farmers who raised the mink in order to slaughter them and use their fur for human clothing and accessories. The entire population was euthanized. An outbreak among wild rabbits occurred simultaneously, killing thousands. Rabbits, hares, jackrabbits, and pikas began succumbing to a different but similar virus causing the rabbits to die of hemorrhagic disease. Rats resorted to cannibalizing their beloved babies, as there was a severe food shortage brought on by restaurant closures and less disposable edible human trash available as humans sheltered in place. Armies of rats confronted other rat kinship formations and battled for resources and territory. Instead of foraging for food at night, rats became daytime scavengers and began attacking other mammals. The desperation was great and overwhelming. The pressure to feed themselves was insurmountable. For rats, that spring was a terrible time of strife and loss.

The virus showed no signs of waning. For a time, everything came to a halt, society was shut down. The curve was lessened, and then returned with a massive second and third wave in some nations, as their societies opened up. There were lasting consequences that the virus presented. People didn't always recover fully. Recurring symptoms were debilitating and strange.

Do you have any recollections? No, well maybe, if so, barely. What I can recall is haloed by a milky haze. Images drift by. I can't attach meanings to the images. I don't feel I should, I don't care to. What are your moods like? My moods are variant, wayward. Similar to the floating images, I don't care to pin down the affective sense of responding one way or another. Someone told me that I reacted chaotically and that they couldn't tell why I might have been triggered. What do you observe? Am I different? Am I altered? From your perspective, do I seem like the person you know? Do I make you uncomfortable? Do you feel disconnected from me? Why do you ask? I sincerely want to know. Taste is connected to sight in ways we don't fully know. Have your daily rhythms shifted? For sure. I never felt like sitting alone in a park before, now I do, regularly. I seem to need more time to process daily life events. But this seems to be generally what many are experiencing, no? I thought I should check in on you more often to see how you are doing. It has been months since you left the hospital. Is it a blur? How are your social relations? Everyone's bandwidth has shrunk. A generalization, I know, but it feels accurate. Some of my closest friends I haven't reached out to, not once. What does that mean? It is as if not seeing someone's mouth move renders them nameless, anonymous, out of the scope of connection. And the strange thing is, it feels normal. Without goodbyes. Simply disconnected. Without the curiosity to probe.

OCEAN

A wave washes up on the shore, fluidic particles like tendrils grazing the grains of sand that collect temporarily along the edge of land and water, the perpetual and constant touch of water and salt and stone and air. The surface area is evidence of touch—so much touching as to cause erosion, and is evidence of coming together, participation. Here there is no separation. This one wave isn't an individual wave that momentarily breaks off from the greater whole and then returns to its collective form, it is the ocean entire, is everything and everyone becoming itself in the constant and cyclical movement of the earth, the moon; it all turns and the tide continues to ebb and flow, and the entire ocean feels itself kissing the sand, like leaving and arriving home over and over again.

There are the oceans that gravitate to earth and the oceans that crest over the treetops. The oceans above the treetops are perpetually in motion, governed by the steady presence of air currents. Trees generate these levitating oceans. They are considered clouds, yet they are very much oceans. Trees mist the air with moisture that they expend from their leaves and in tall stands the moisture clings to particles and rides on the wind. It is possible to see hovering oceans fly in the sky, over continents. Skyward oceans break the barrier between the psyche's various divisions. Oceans that are able to climb into the skies are light and air-bound, saturated with dew from water that has climbed up through tree trunks and then becomes aerosolized into the atmosphere. The lakes, rivers, and oceans that are formed this way are crucial for large intersectional organisms to survive. A stand of trees here will send an ocean to their stationary relatives there. Gestures are always reciprocal and generous. A major role trees play is to create moving bodies of water.

Birds on long migratory journeys will fly through a hovering ocean to get nourishment; birds don't have to land on earth to drink moisture—they can simply fly on a route with a cloud-bound ocean. The health of the planet is determined by these motion-filled oceans delivering their load of hydrogen and oxygen to plants and trees that need the liquid.

The oceans are atmosphere and feeling. The feeling is of root systems and dirt and worms as well as mushrooms and all the reciprocal energy that these organisms share. While the water is organized as a cloud, the moving ocean is an organism. Once the water falls back to earth, the organism disperses into many droplets. Lucidity is the mind state of these oceans that go where moisture is necessary. Prophetic of rain, the sky ocean delivers its load on expectant soils and plants and other organisms that need water to thrive.

Water is a transient state. Water becomes gaseous and also freezes into ice hard as rock. In order to understand water, it is important to think of the role water plays within the organism's cellular structure. Water holds consciousness temporarily in place.

I love this: they flock together at the ocean's edge, a perimeter made unclear by the cold and by the wind whipping up sand and snow. It is freezing, it is difficult to be together or be apart. They press their bodies into another. They gesticulate with their arms. Their spines form one column. There are five couples. They seem exchangeable in that their identities are unknown and unremarkable. The performance has no viewers except the ocean, the sand, the sky, themselves, the choreographer. The time of day is unclear; the sun isn't visible except as diffused light. They take off and put on their jackets, parkas, this is part of the performance. They flail and scurry. Their bodies merge and separate. When together, there is excitement in their movements. Bodies echo one another. Closeness is evident. The ocean breathes with them. They are smaller vessels, also oceans. They are in tandem with oceanic expansiveness. The dance movements are simple. What you can do together with another body is expressional and there are seemingly endless iterations. They care about the ocean and the ocean cares about them, the planetary state of equilibrium. Care in this case is not bound by emotion—it is something else. The gorgeousness of the moment translates into light and shadow, figure and relief. Relief is as grand as figure. Both are in motion. There is no stillness. The light, though it is opaque, is moving.

A snail begins to know this world by starting from the mud, where it all starts, up and down soft leaves, across the rough concrete to find how worthless time really is. The girl remembers the murky matter, remembers not to look away, remembers that the time before is neither reason created or recovered and the expected disaster has already and will already arrive all too soon, is already here, was never here in the first place. A disaster, how? Why?

In a dream the girl travels through a vigilant portal to find herself in the first primordial ocean, a melancholic and deep place, a murky and fluidic place of possibility, murmurous and beautiful and monstrous in its too-muchness that will only collapse and expand with attention. She swims in the water, trying to make meaning from her own stare; her human gaze in these depths is intrusive. The giant creatures swim past her and she feels the power of their presence, the strength of their stride as they slice through the water and create currents that push her outward toward what seems like becoming, becoming, more becoming. She swims past the tiny creatures that her human eyes don't know to sense, she feels them against her skin, against her sight, the kelp forest moving to a rhythm she can't hear, but her body senses it too somehow. Are they all moving together? She wants to touch everything, know everything. She wants to keep this all in her memory, take it back with her. When she wakes, she won't remember, but will carry a feeling in the plates of her bones and the flutters of her feet as she kicks and pretends she is a dolphin in the water. "Look at me, I'm a dolphin!" she will scream in delight. Her mother will nod and acknowledge the little sea creature splashing in the tub, water and suds everywhere. What is the route away from here?

The ocean is often responsible for our worst nightmares. Oceanic depth is unfathomable. The water pressure at the depth of the ocean causes extreme compression. Lungs and bones will break at such depths. But few have experienced these traumas so why would the ocean cause fright? The ocean is responsible for demonstrably changing the world and how society functions. Once trees were chopped down in primordial forests, huge galleons were constructed, forever altering the social patterns of humans and other floral and faunal life. With the ability to travel over great expanses of water, humans and other animals could go everywhere, and with this fluidity of travel came a more pervasive dispersal of ideas and ideologies. There was no retracting what happened when transportation by sea became the standard. Irrevocable damage was done to humans and habitats. Millions of people were kidnapped, forced onto ships, forced into slave labor. Bodies were hurled off of ships into the salty frothing waves, bringing to bear a condition of perpetual mourning. The oceans hold this grief and struggle. Value takes on different meanings that shift constantly. One's life could be in dire jeopardy in this new calculus. With the large ships truly everything became aggrandized and larger, and what was considered negligible and less became thought of as expendable to the point of brutality, barbarity—how people were treated, how the ecology was treated.

The girl remembers the primordial state of being in the womb, unborn, cramped in her mother's uterus. She remembers the time she grew a tail and the tail then matured into her sitz bone. She remembers the flexing of her spine and her knees as she floated in the womb. And now when she visits the ocean, the feeling of being primordially unborn comes back to her. Out of the navel of history. Feeling womblike is a feeling of enchantment. Feeling enchantment is a state of grace. She wears the legacy of the horror in her bones. The ocean conveys repressed emotions. Visualizing, she sees the longest mountain ranges on earth under the water. There are deep chasms, and immense volcanoes, muddy silty sand flat for miles along the ocean's floor. A narwhal and a grampus swim by. A school of silvery fish swarms her mind's eye. They flash by in a second, a mirror of light blinding her, shocking her senses. The saltiness of her skin beckons her to the sea. Her blood tastes of iron and mineral ions and hormones. Seawater is replete with bromine and magnesium, chloride, and sodium, also potassium. Fluoride and boron are present. There are dissolved atmospheric gasses in seawater: argon, carbon dioxide, oxygen, and nitrogen. Other elements become dispersed by the thermohaline and wind-driven circulation, using the combinatorial structure of ocean water. Rivers pump dissolved particulates into oceans creating mixed mediums. Corrosive substances leech out.

The girl leaves the house in the morning: what is to be confirmed or made sacred in the memory of her own birth, of this lifetime and the many before?

The girl hopes to remain on this earth for quite a while longer: what is the fate that she accepted when, in a previous life, she stood on that giant ship, sensing the emanations of the ocean and sky to detect masses of land and other ships from impossible distances—the dream-pursuit of nauscopy—and the bodies thrown overboard for the fish; where are those bodies now, and who has fed on them? The ocean is an ancestor.

The girl cries out in the night: what is the nature of ritual when she is always swimming in her dreams and always drowning in the afternoons? The work of great beauty or nothing at all—why always this polarized dichotomy, why always one or the other?

The dandelions are prophesizing as the girl leaves the house in the morning and the dandelions expand their presence outward from the fields, the gardens, the cities, in the girl's hair. What greater expansion of the present than when the wind blows mightily and an ocean of dandelion seeds, billions and trillions of cypselae float in the air to cover the world with new, tiny worlds, worlding, becoming—here futures contained in the movement of the wind, the conditions of the sky, humans leaving their homes in the morning to witness the wind.

She now lives by the ocean and every day she approaches the shore to see what the ocean has regurgitated from deep in its belly. There are crabs and jellyfish and pieces of various organisms' bodies, unidentifiable except as a specific mass of tissue. The ocean produces smells that unsettle the body. A salty rotten smell is primal. Such a smell can cause a violent reaction. There are sweet rotten smells also, of blood and slime that combine as scent, signaling decay. Kelp smells vivid green, primordial, and conveys a sensation of growth and entanglement. Stones that have rolled over sand also smell piquant, like sulfur, like sweat and heat. The sand smells of urine and sometimes feces and sometimes like burning hair. She sits on the sand and also rolls in it and tries to unwind out of grief and longing. The water rushes up against her. She is totally rock face and infallible. The next moment she is nauseous because of the sun and the smell of oil, a toxin she can fathom with the slightest intake of breath. The oil was dredged many miles away and reeks of acrid death. She needs the ocean, and she is also fearful of the ocean in a way that she isn't frightened of anything else, not even death. The ocean wants to take her out; she feels its tug. She could relent, whimsically. She could let go and be swept away, never to return to land. The ocean makes her realize she loves life but doesn't care to let go of it. She could give her life to the ocean, so sensuous and grand. She could be pulled in and she is certain her body would become food almost immediately. On land she might rot, in the ocean she would be eaten part by part. Tiny single-celled worms would eat her hair. Giant sharks would eat her bones.

She wouldn't leave a trace. She would become ocean—a translucency—within a day. She pulls back, moves onto the shore so that the waves can no longer reach her.

She needs to arrive at a decision. She will wait. The ocean is a time clock and reminds her of breath and the moon. Breath is contingent on lung intake and the waves are contingent on the moon's gravitational pull, surging like breath. She imagines dying here, today. She resists. Others have died here. She sees evidence of death all around. The body becomes food, this is the way flesh is reordered. The ocean can transform objects into pure life. Potentiality is translucent wave particles. The presence of phosphorescent beings attracts her.

The moment that you fall into the ocean you remember what it feels like to fall, to let go, to hold back, to arrive and be surrounded.

The joy and nausea of a dandelion seed floating in the wind.

The tree gives dictation and, on the wind, hears everything: in the distance, rumbling waves, gathering whales, so many bones at the bottom of the sea.

Scampering feet on the rooftops. For humans, once the knee is bent, there is a whole symbology that must come to light. For squirrels, everything that is sacred is also buried in the dirt, to be sought for later.

Crows may witness squirrels and the building of their archives. In the field, collaboration and competition are not distinct phenomena.

The prophecy of the dandelions was to expand and so the squirrels spread nuts and berries perpetually.

(The girl remembers the crying of baby squirrels in the attic at night, her mother reporting to the landlord about a hole in the house somewhere, that there were squirrels living inside and could he patch up the hole to prevent future contamination of wildlife? It was not her intent, but it was the consequence of her desire for boundaries, to keep out what, in her opinion, did not belong *inside* the house: an exterminator was called and there were no more baby squirrels crying in the attic at night.)

The prophecy is in the movement of tiny feet on the roof. The prophecy is in the burial of acorns in the dirt, organized by date, an archive of nature's own readiness to be consumed. The prophecy is in the memory of where they all are buried, the recognition of trees, the knowing of the distance between themselves, the tree, their bodies, movements in the winds. Like a form of nauscopy, the squirrel detects acorns at impossible distances, sensing the daily character of the sky, the rain, the fungal terrain underground, the different smell of each and every nut buried in countless patches all across the land.

In the final ocean, the last ocean that will ever exist before the first one, there lies an acorn buried beneath the sand at the bottom of an unfathomable body of water, an acorn buried there for the future. Some distance away, a squirrel lifts his face up to the wind, nose twitching and catching the scent of salt and tannin. About that acorn lying in wait, *This isn't the time yet*, the squirrel thinks to himself.

The ocean archives the past by transforming matter into translucency. The ocean breaks everything down to the smallest denominator. The ocean generates an autonomous sensory meridian response and with it, a flickering and a spectral jolt that conducts electricity through cells and incites the becoming of nothing like when stars burst or when things come in and out of being.

Jittery, wobbly shivers. The original ocean and the final ocean vie for attention. They overlay one another so we see through one to the other. The future taints the present if you stress out about what will happen next. This is how worlds bleed into each other. The past bloats the future with expenditure. Now the trees are filled with flowers, and everything is becoming its future self and seeding and creating the possibility of another iteration.

The ocean wants a final hand in all matters. Salt is a final form. Salt is a preserver. To be interned in salt is to rest forever. Salt is a conductor of electricity. Cows enjoy licking salt. Mammals tend to enjoy salty things. The clouds have saline in them. Saltwater chokes out the flora by the shore. The waves crest and kill off the tender growths. Other sea plants thrive on salty brine. Razor-sharp grasses that grow twelve feet high thrive on it. Egrets with puffy plumage plunge their beaks into the brackish water, for fish and crabs are in abundance in the murky silt. The sun sets and looks as if it were the cause of a nuclear meltdown and, as a star, that is essentially what is happening. Is she becoming a red giant or a white pulsar? The squirrels are burying nuts out of season, what does this mean? There was an abundance of nuts, and they are busy burying them in spring. All around, oak seedlings sprout. The rocks are igneous and have experienced compression and the force of deep earth. They yawn as rocks do—slowly, altering the ego of the dirt.

One squirrel has eaten something he is unfamiliar with, and it has caused him to feel dizzy and unsure, so he avoids trees. He makes his way to a cellar hole and rests there. He signals to his family, *Whatever you do don't eat what I just ate, it might be poisonous.* He has to wait it out, ride the strangeness of metabolism. A strange morsel.

The occasional question that one might have is, how is language so broken, how are the sentences so inadequate for the dictations that occur in the shadows, the insistence of individual humanity amidst all of this catastrophe? The ocean posits happening as happening, that is, a body of water is affected by planetary bodies that also create gravity for animal bodies who insist on creating textual bodies, and the water, like a mother carrying a child across a field to protect it from predators, only knows to surround and receive.

Nothing is broken, says the water. Because nothing is meant to be fixed. Because cause and effect ignore the significance of shadows. Because there are enough nuts for everyone but not enough foresight. Because there is always risk but risk assessment borders on a categorical pinning-down. Morality, if there are only two sides, is for suckers. In another space and time, there is a squirrel who tracks the scent of an acorn long-buried in the ocean. In this one, a squirrel tracks the salty scent of preserved fish. This isn't in his usual diet, but he accesses memory of a future life and is drawn to it; the allure is stomach-churning, but he feels his nose tremble. The other squirrels are not prepared, he is not prepared, and this fish isn't for them, and yet this future memory has charged itself in this moment, and this particular moment of harm will also become a past memory for that future self, because memories are entangled like the molecules of water.

A sacred occult map is the only way the acorn can be located and recovered from the ocean and when there is the realization that the ocean is internal as it is external, two parts of the same whole, spatial dimensions bend oddly. To find the way back or into somewhere requires a relenting, a giving up and succumbing not in defeat but in recognition. Reabsorption. If you don't allow yourself to slip out of your membrane you will always be an impersonation of reality. Maybe impersonation isn't the right description of this phenomenon. It is ok to stay within the membrane as an option. Maybe seed is better. Gestating but never popping open the membrane. In death the action is done for you. It happens automatically. You don't have to try. You will rot or burn or be eaten. You will change form. There are rigors involved and risks. Maps leading out of oneself into another are available. You won't resume in the exact same form. You might feel out of sorts, a bit confused. Speaking alternative languages. Speaking oddly. The body transforms as it ages. The skin wants to shed, prefers to wrinkle. And you look at the wrinkled person and might feel awe. You may not notice all the people who are old and wrinkled and have a different sensibility.

The squirrel was old, and his arm was broken, and climbing was rough-going. Very rough-going. Twice he fell out of a tree. He managed to catch a branch both times. He couldn't fight other squirrels for food—he had to wait it out and get the nuts that were bruised or moldy. He ate more moldy food, and this affected sensation and perception. He was ignored by his family circle. The trees dropped more acorns this year than ever in his memory and his strength was improving. He was feeling livelier and was able to get about the tree trunks with agility. He ate as much as he could to fortify himself. He dreamed as many hours as he could. The longer he dreamed the more energy he had. He encountered a badger, and he encountered an eagle, lately. He also came into contact with rabbits, rats, and field mice. He noticed numerous crows. There were many to greet and acknowledge.

Oceans are intent on expansion—they will envelop land if the conditions are right. When temperatures rise, water molecules expand, thus the sheer volume of water expands. Sea levels are rising. Ice is melting. Warm oceans chew at the ice. Ancient ice contains minerals and is darker in coloration. When exposed to the sun, the dark layers melt quicker. Each subsequent layer of ice melts at an increasingly rapid pace. The oceans are interested in primordial beginnings, beginning again, a new beginning after many starts and die-offs. A repetition of beginnings and beginning again. All water bodies prefer to run toward the oceans if conditions are right. The saltiness is a draw. The sheer distribution of the volume of water is magnetic. Water is heavier than ice—denser. A maximum density in liquid form. Water is thought of as the stage of hiding and is associated with bones and ears. The moon and water commingle. It feels as if time moves in peculiar fashion—the ocean regulates time with the moon, recalibrating the mistaken rhythms, the breaths out of sequence. Rising outside the dualism of good and evil, the ocean's turbulence is beyond moral bounds. The triangle is the alchemical symbol for water. The word for "emerald" and the word for "water" are the same in ancient Egyptian language. Salts and minerals dissolve in water, contributing to the ocean's chemistry. The acidity or alkalinity of the ocean fluctuates. Responding teasingly, the ocean swishes mammoth tonnages of liquified ions that become waves. If anyone can predict the future, it is the ocean.

UPRISING

If anyone can transform toward an emergent us, it is the collective. Sweaty, congruous, bold.

The expression of the trees is an incantatory and imaginative type, almost ominous, almost encouraging you to stay distant from the beauty but beckoning you toward everything that is offered by the earth. Contradictory only in language. In the woods, in the marketplace, by the river, the ghosts rise up out of the soil, down from the sky, gathering, wisps of energy like smoky entrails that curl up and seize the air. Key words: gathering, dispersing.

How does one unbind herself from the burdens and mistakes of her ancestors? How does one not pass back her own wounds to her ancestral lineage? If time is simultaneous, how do the past and present and future commingle in this space, the scar tissue that reveals itself in the mowing of lawns, in the burying of nuts in the ground, in the flapping of wings, in the decimation of bees, in the spreading of strawberry plants, in the constant breath, in that feeling of powerlessness that resides beneath your feet, all of it illusory and entangled and ephemeral and necessary and present.

Uprising: what are the actions associated with rising from the grave? Isn't that the birth of all living beings, all new births stemming from the compost and grief and mulched remains of our ancestors? Isn't uprising just a branch of decomposition, and isn't the blue window through which we look out longingly just another expression of the system that continues to imprison us?

The bluish miner bees start to buzz above the compost. Scraps of food were thrown onto their hive, unbeknownst to the person throwing the food. The bees are furtive, prefer their familial circle, are shy of the earth's other inhabitants. The offense bothers them, but they do not sting the assailant. They fly about and then head back to the propolis, and their queen. Helicopters whir overhead. Another threat, another struggle happening simultaneously. Militarized, the helicopter no doubt has ammunition pointed at the protesters. The uprising, the virus, and the ocean come together in an epic formation. The virus highlights the inequity that persists since the creation of a social organization called "the nation," stolen, brutally wrested from other people who were castigated from land, lifeways. Now, the uprising addresses the energy of the wound, the crisis, the transfer of memory to frontline action. The virus, a threat and reminder, plays a part as timely as the collective need to transform violence to community care. Burying shameful action will only create a stronger, bolder uprising. Fortifying a system that generates perpetual grief will only backfire. The present presents an opportunity for clarification and action. The virus, as a kind of timeless code, becomes generative in bodies, an interpolated spark.

The streets were filled with plangent cries. Every utterance is utopic. Every utterance is blasphemy to a power structure that thrives on a racialized hierarchy, where prisons are an integral part of the economic infrastructure. Every cry to alter hegemonic strategy is a cry for a feasible reworlding. The virus shows us how we affect each other. The virus demonstrates how susceptible we are. History's linearity is disrupted by the virus and the uprising. Together the virus and the uprising envision a different way of living.

The power of the uprising is the power of every spirit that has already existed before, all of the ghosts, of all of the beings, every being that marches accompanied by thousands more, luminous energy fields like giant glowing masses. The virus reveals how much hatred is still living there, always in the name of reason, always in the name of progress. How has everyone forgotten how permeable we are?

Squirrel got your ear? A fuzzy dissonance. An overload. We might have slipped through a crevice in the cracking. Where, the fissures? What frequencies? Who is talking? The squirrel, without the access to the kind of language we expect, asks if the humans might find a way of being in the world without being dependent on their exclusionary paradigms. Everywhere *humans, humans, humans;* here now, squirrels. As pets they would be incorporated into the human family. As rather cute rodents, we exist in a liminal position, pest and mascot. That is, for the humans, those great apes of refinement who cultivate intimacy as their inclinations suit them.

Remember the complexities of *Biosphere 2*?—with the disastrous assumption that a *Biosphere 1*, the Earth, has even existed. The ego behind such an assertion, that there is a cohesive, stable, self-contained world that can be expressed in the first place. Earth is not a vivarium, as the cosmos touches it. In Oracle, Arizona, one can study the forensics of an aftermath. One can also watch reruns of *Big Brother* and realize the complex shitstorm of microcosmic interrelations when humans are contained within an enclosure isolated from the world, worlds. Where is the closed settlement that the humans keep dreaming of? They travel further and further, sending ships, even cars, into space, looking for that fantasy of closure. What might be labeled as "the anthropos imaginary" is an ironic magical thinking. That as humans, we believe we act from a place of freedom. We act as if we are not entangled in that which we act upon. The virus already knows how it fits into the larger web of things. The crow flaps his wings and riles up the squirrel trying to cross an electric wire. The dandelions spread their seeds, and a human wonders what is the best way to remove moss from her roof, what is the best way to get rid of the pests leaving holes in the strawberries in her garden, what is the best way to keep her house intact and clean and sterile, what is the best to support the uprising in the streets, what is the best way to let her friends know that she is doing her best to support the uprising in the streets. The visible uprising is a performance. The invisible one is in the air, in the soul, the dancing ghosts provoking the slugs to eat all of the chard. Is there anything "wrong" with this picture? Why does anything have to be wrong?

Binaries lead to break down, always. Yes, electricity contains positive and negative ions but when worlding a paradigm, it is vital to imagine the boundaries between forces breaking down.

Imagine placing your nemesis's joy at the center of a circle. Imagine the circle growing ever larger. Imagine watering the circle. Contemplate living in the circle, adding seeds to the circle. Now imagine the circle being struck by a force—what does the force represent? Have you been duly represented by this action? What countermeasure will equate a potent response? Power thrives on binaries. Power would like *you* to stand here and shut up, do the dirty work, and it demands *you* forget your boredom by spending money on trivial junk made of the body of the Earth. The hands of power come by and strangulate, contaminate, command. We say *no* and revolt and the hands ignore the protest. What eludes power is the strength of the collective. The uprising will succeed. Power will be redistributed. The ocean will redraw the outline of the nation-state. The squirrels are resting in the trees because it is midafternoon, and they, with their babies, are snoozing, and the miner bees are incubating. Photosynthesis is all around, transforming energy, and for once the military helicopters are silent. The nation is "reopening." The virus is doing something indecipherable.

The virus:

/

/ // ///// . /

/ // . ,

,

. / ;

"

/

/ "

.

/ /// ,

. ^

!

The uprising is the dispersal of dandelion seeds in the air.
The uprising is a squirrel remembering all of the acorns he buried months before.
The uprising is the labor of earthworms.
The uprising is the formation of mycorrhizal networks underground.
The uprising is the bowl of water set out on the altar for the ancestors.
The uprising is the resurrection of moss after a long rain.
The uprising is compost and decomposition.
The uprising is falling, then remembering to get up again.
The uprising is the actions of you, all of your ghosts, all of your dead, all of your ancestors, all of your wounds, all of your gifts, all of your past and present and future entangled in the present moment.
The uprising is the act of rising up from the grave, even after you are dead.
The uprising is knowing that the blue window through which you look longingly isn't the way to freedom but another expression of the system that perpetuates your imprisonment.

A human washes the dishes and her hands are getting wrinkly. She scrubs the pot twice to make sure she didn't miss any spots, and then notices the tips of her fingers, the ridges and lines that indicate where the water has permeated her body. How much of the grease from the pot has entered her body through her fingers? How much of her own fluids have leaked out into the sink, down the drain, back out into the rivers and oceans? She doesn't remember the last time she has cried. She has cried too many times today.

Constellations of breath. Here in the city that lost over 20,000 people to the virus, the long snaking marches of the protestors aren't funerary, and yet, they are. There are those that doubt the deaths. The deaths are real. The marches are real and, most importantly, the demands are real. With every death the uprising grows. When he cried, "I can't breathe," the power structure didn't acknowledge the suffering but the many did hear and respond. "I can't breathe," is a rally cry. The bodies and spirits of the protestors form an endless line that weaves its way through the city. The pattern dies out and regroups, dies out and reassembles. Every day. The police kettle and arrest and the protesters come again. The protesters won't be quelled. The mayor can make an edict in the form of a curfew and place seven thousand police on the streets, but it will not mute the protestors. Listening is a form of attention. Listening is how two entities acknowledge each other. If you aren't listening, you are locked in a solipsistic world and perhaps the universe is not real in your reality. That's why there is clapping, shouting, and, at times, screaming, because we can see that you refuse to listen. It is nearly summer and sound waves become louder in the heat. The sound of protest intensifies. Summer will drive these points home. Home, you might ask, is where? Earth. This shared Earth. Extractivism doesn't understand reciprocity. The piercing decibels of sound cannons, the particular sound of pepper spray being projected onto a crowd, the snap of batons on people's backs. In one city, an elderly man was knocked off his feet by the police. In one city, two college students were pepper sprayed point-blank while they sat in their car and were then dragged out and pinned to the ground. In one city, a protester, trying to get away from a cloud of tear gas was fired at with a rubber bullet, fracturing her eye socket. The sounds of footsteps, the sounds of fluttering banners, the sounds of reassurance amongst the protesters. The tone of the message, the tone of the sirens, the tone of your voice through your facemask. The sound of chanting and messaging: "Black Lives Matter," "In Defense of Black Life," "Housing is Healthcare," Defund the Police," "Burn it Down," "Justice Calls for a Copless Future," "Compliance Won't Keep You Safe," "Racism is a Pandemic Too." The feel of the asphalt, the feel of your arm holding a placard, the feel of collective action, the feel of demonstration, the feeling of fury and rage, love, and peace. Signs are stenciled on ragged cardboard, on hand-painted placards, on huge banners. "Who Can I Call When the Murderer Wears a Badge?" "Stop Killing Us," "Demilitarize the Police," "Don't Shoot," "Am I Next?" "White Silence = Death," "Smash White Supremacy," "I Can't Breathe," "I Am Not a Threat," "Hands Up, Don't Shoot," "We Are Sacred." Collective emotion is tumultuous and wild.

Feeling runs through the cranium into the base of the neck, grounding into the soles of feet. Hands feel electric and teeth are clenched and unclenched as the mood varies. Extreme claustrophobia and the joy of being together are not mutually exclusive in the time of the virus and in the time of the uprising. Everything is tentative and pulsating. Some of the protests coil through major portions of the city, some are tiny and intense. The sound of rain and the sound of melting ice. The sound of deep inhalation and gasping for breath. Say goodbye to that outdated model because the world is changing, as birds are dispersing the seeds from last year's blooms.

The birds fly over the protestors and don't see frogs nor sky, but blooms and linkages. The ground is burnt, which accounts for the change in texture, a change in focus. The way one sends messages has changed. There aren't words, just ashes. No drought, just thirst. No desire, just dispersion. Freedom can be found in proximity and those who feel whole are the first to be eaten. The sounds are deafening. They can't be heard but felt, explosive pulses through one's skeletal framework, the shaking of one's entire body, are your ears bleeding or is that water that someone has thrown at you because of the tear gas? Are you crying or has your body become an improbability? The image of death is splayed out on the bottom of someone's shoe, and no one can remember that there was blood everywhere when they were born. The birds don't have imperfect breaths, just uneven ones. And when they fly, the sounds around them are felt in their hearts, human wrists like putty just fall apart and the birds still roost and watch. What is personal property in a time like this? A protestor shares his supplies with another protestor. Were these his supplies to begin with? Is the act of sharing so radical? Why do we depend so much on "his" and "hers" and "my" and "me?"

Describe your body if you can. This isn't an exercise, but a test. This isn't a test but it's definitely homework. If you don't have a home then there is no homework, just remember to breathe. The protestors all chant out: *I can't breathe.*

There is a melting point, a turning point and change of direction. *Now* delineates how the future is a construct based on desire and vision. *Now* shows us how our bodies form a continuum. The future is cobbled together out of the scar tissue, traumatic wounds, and insight culled from yesterday's undercurrents. How to heal collective wounds? This is the collective work that the world hopes to undertake. Forget retiring on Mars. This is the planet of war. One need not go to Mars to encounter devastation. If you have a thirst for violence, you have arrived. Your wounds indicate that you are home. Wounds are incredible complications. A wound is hard to see, hard to look at. At once it seems disrespectful to look at another's wound up close and yet, it is heartless not to. And you can't simply look, once you know of the suffering there is a responsibility to assuage the pain. How many layers of skin will grow over an unhealed wound? Have we been going about healing in an indirect way? What are the ways that healing can take place? A healthcare system that deals with collective trauma on a mass scale. A healthcare that addresses intergenerational violence and racism. A healthcare that caringly, lovingly nurtures, lets the pus run out, lets the scab grow again. More people will die from the virus and from the menacing system that is fortified by violence. More people are standing up to the system that rewards obsequiousness. Violence is the revival of monocultural domination. Splendid diversities of trees die out in a monoculture; splendid diversities of insects die out in a monoculture. A monoculture requires toxic nutrients and industrial attention. Monocultural industries pay the skimpiest wages and are willing to sacrifice workers. As hazardous as these jobs are, they are made invisible. The state doesn't grant citizenship to the people who garden on an industrial scale to feed the nation. Hidden by plumes of acrid chemicals, the workers tend the vegetables. The ocean roils and the ice caps melt, and before us is an unprecedented scenario for human minds maturing at the pace of a fabricated matrix of toil. The marching is redundant and necessary. Marching and yelling the same messages again and again into the wind, into the sky, into the other marcher's hair and skin. Tomorrow. The day after and again. Different people, the same people. A different street, the same street. Thudding repetition. New feeling. New energy. New dire necessities, the same dire necessities. A tautology of necessity and deliberation. With sounds and movement in the sun, exposed to the state. We have a glimpse of the possibilities we are capable of.

Wound: I am not —
Virus: remain, want, friend
Wound: It is death, everywhere.
Virus: sky, remain, sky

What I fear
can be found in the forest
An unbreathing
person still identifies with the sky
Constantly on the edge
only if you see it that way
Burnt ground, broken heart
it is only death
isn't it?
it is

The circulation of sounds is such that bodies are listening to an average of two hundred seventy-one conversations at any given time, conversations between other humans in their vicinity, conversations between the birds, between the worms, between the plants, between the spirits, between the wind and the sky. Listening, of course, doesn't only happen with the ears, though it helps if your ears are not bleeding. It helps if you are breathing. It helps if you know how to breathe with your heart, in addition to your lungs, in addition to your belly. It helps if you've offered some of your eyelashes to the plants and it helps if you've had your green juice in the morning. *Friend, I'm reaching out to say hello to you. Are you there listening?*

They are listening. They hear the vibrations. They smell your presence. They crowd together to be together and welcome you into their fold. Hello! Perhaps it is difficult to notice them. They live at a different threshold. Their life frame creates a different timescale. Hello! They nonetheless call out, exuberant. Hello! They are at the threshold of life and death and there is a lot of traffic at the intersection. Hello! You know instinctively that they are listening and responding because you are able to sense color, smell, hear sounds—they regulate your emotions, they regulate your intake of stimuli. Hello! Every day they offer a greeting and also calm you to sleep. Every day they activate your taste buds, your glands, give you the sensation of excitement. They are together with you as a body that you ironically think of as yours alone. They are as much your body as you think you are an individualized self. They don't need praise or attention. They will do their work regardless. They want smell, touch, and hearing to radiate among bodies. They calibrate how internal and external reality bonds. History is a collaboration at this microscale. Hello! Hello! Hello!

We are listening. We sense the vibrations. We smell your presence. Hm, yes. We crowd together to be together and welcome you into our fold. Hello! Greetings! Welcome! Perhaps it is difficult to notice us, though we are everywhere, around you, in the cracks, at the edges, in the folds. Hello! We are calling out. Hello! We are watching you and know that you will hear us soon. We are patient and persistent. We are with you, and you are never alone. We are as much your body as you think you are an individualized self. We are you. You are us. Isn't this collaboration beautiful? We are here for you. We don't need praise or attention. Hello! Again, hello! We will do our work regardless. So will you. And in this way, we will always be together. Forever. And ever. And ever...

In the area were many species of trees. The trees canopied the roadway. Mosses draped over the branches. A sleepy community by the coast. A mid-spring day. Sunshine glowing on leaves and reflecting off the pavement. Seemingly peaceful, harmonious.

How to register harmony, peace? How to calibrate an undertone of unrest? Unrest and or distress. Distress has mutated across centuries and reacts to the forms of ever-present violence. A fully loaded atmosphere that triggers the worst human impulse. Rises from the balls of the feet to the gut to the cerebellum and back to the throat, the gut, returning to the earth, the soil. A young man decided to jog down a street he is familiar with as he lives here. Solo, with the wind, in harmony with trees that give him oxygen, energy. He diverts his attention briefly to an abandoned house. He thinks maybe he can find a drink of water. He enters the house and leaves it again in minutes. Neighbors across the street notice his entry and exit. They jump in their pickup truck. They tell their friend to join them. There is a father and a son and their friend. They pursue the young man. They ride after him. They ride after a violent history of such pursuits. They become an echo in an echo chamber of violence. They are possessed by a vision of themselves that is incompatible with others. Their vision of themselves surpasses rationality. They succumb to a built-up fabrication that had taken centuries to develop and deploy. The father and son are fueled by something so deep and persistent as to motivate them to stalk this young man, and when they encounter him, their impulse is to kill him. Shoot him point blank with a shotgun. To understand this act is to understand a nation and its tools of oppression. Tools of oppression that have become organ tissue, internalized, growing subcutaneously. Bigger than the men but exactly in their proportion. The paradigm of hate persists.

Hello!

The trees, gripping the earth, are witness, always witnessing human actions. The sky is a dome of consciousness. The death of the young man creates a sadness that feeds into a creative response of outrage. The young man becomes everyone's memory, everyone's ghost.

Hello!

The thing is, everyone has a trail of ghosts following them around everywhere they go, they're just not always aware of it. Or they haven't dealt with their own wounds in order to be able to face the ghosts. So, they just trail behind, helpless, pandering, sometimes wailing, an infinite-day grieving process of repeated cries that last until the order is given to stop, sometimes anger, the habitual raising of a knife and lowering it down over and over again, whether there is a body beneath the blade, whether the blade is sharp enough, whether anyone deserves anything, whether it all makes sense. The problem with a sense of justice is that it relies on a sense of morality, and the problem with morality is that it relies on whether actions are just or unjust, right or not right, deserved or undeserved. Meritocracy within ethics reinforces the paradigms of power, not of balance or alignment, so when the blade is raised, when the sight is on the target, when one's hands are pressed against another's neck, when one strings up rope around a tree branch, the rationale of whether someone deserved to die because they did something wrong comes down to the wrongness of the body, the wrongness of power misplaced, the wrongness of status quo disturbed. Anything can be justified. All of it. And the dandelions continue spreading their seeds, seeds in the wind that float past the bodies, getting stuck in wisps of hair, on the backs of walking dogs, on the paws of squirrels, in the corners of potted plants on porches.

Hello!

The place where the squirrels, the potted plants, the trees with the mossy canopies, and the men, both father and son duo plus their friend and the young man, live is a place proliferating with ghosts and ghosting narratives. Nothing superficial will do when the stressors run so deep and the crevices are so many. The paradoxes have to be teased apart and the morality of the questions dissolved in nectar, serum, or oceanic saline. The first reality is that in the present, people who are the original inhabitants are forced to pay for housing, for food, for ecological situatedness—the houses, food, and ecological whole that previously they lived within, nurtured, understood as home. Previously there wasn't a culture of exchange that projected extractive value onto each thing, each item, each commodity. People who lived here didn't own the land because no one can own the Earth. *Hello!* They are then told that they must buy the land and everything they need to live. This is the first paradox and until it is understood no other layered paradox will unwind. Converting a shared reality into a commodified thing rewires place. Home takes on a different connotation when there is a mediating structure based on profit and commerce. This new system is enforced by a military apparatus stronger than any previously encountered. How is it possible for people arriving somewhere, who know nothing about the place they are arriving to, to tell those already living there that everything they share is no longer sharable? In fact, every transaction must now go through the banks, lawyers, and the police.

Are you still in the vicinity?

I am going home. This house, this land is mine, I bought it. By the time I get home, you better be off of my property. One man utters these statements out loud. This is the way of things. What is earned and owed and deserved. Morality at work again. Take away possession, though, and what might the shift be?

We are all home. We are grateful to have the support and shelter of this structure upon the generous land. We honor the land. We are always already home. Therefore, you are always already welcome.

Imagine owning nothing. Imagine life without the concept of ownership even. Imagine the spirit within everything, all of the spirits intermingling. Not the trail of ghosts that follows, an accumulation of sorrows and regrets and wounds stuck in the linearity of progress, like a garbage dump that only grows and magnifies as more is consumed, and time moves forward like an error, but an entanglement of spirit, the mycelial network awakened by the push and pull of all living beings, as an animal is killed its carcass feeds many, and then the fungi work and the body is returned to the soil. The process of death is also always the process of life, and like wisps of smoke we are constantly in the process of touching everything else. A squirrel sits atop a beheaded and mutilated tree.

Can you feel my breath? Can you feel me sitting here? Because I can feel your loss. And my perching here is a way to acknowledge your pain, your loss. And my scampering away is my way to acknowledge the cycles of life and death, of violence. And my movement across the grass is my way to acknowledge all of our journeys across the stars.

The wind is stirring. Can you feel it too?

The muskrats and possums dart across a huge open lawn that is dotted with rocks and monoliths. Smooth rock faces inscribed with names and dates of birth and death. The expanse of mowed lawn with the rock faces is an excellent place to forage for delicious spring clover and dandelion. The grasses haven't seeded and are tender. Rabbits are here with their litters. The animals stick together in their familial groups, they are familiar with each other, cohabitate, and give each other space. They run over the dead. They nourish themselves on the nutrients coming up from the ground through the roots of the grasses they munch on. All the Vietnam veterans, all the veterans of the Korean War, all the veterans of World War I and World War II, their bones already mulched. The spouses and sisters and brothers of these soldiers resting by their side are changing into soil. When they come on some days, there are flags fluttering, and they are astounded at how many soldiers are resting here. The Gulf Wars, the war in Afghanistan, proxy wars, cold wars. The untold deaths of Native people who were killed during the formation of the nation-state. The untold deaths of people who toiled under unfreedom to build the infrastructure of this system. The microorganisms that arrive don't care if they were soldiers; the nutritious elements of their bodies are equal. There is an atmosphere of transformation. The traumatic content from the lives of the people resting here is now mineral and energetic. The sorrow is converted. The muskrats and possums are eager to eat as much clover as they can ingest and then, rest by a little forest stream. Humans come by and mow the epic spaces. The forest remains untouched by humanity for now. Humans are afraid of ticks and other small insects. They stay within the manicured plots and, even then, they barely visit the slick stone faces. The stones themselves are from far-off global points. Different substances, different chemical compounds. Lichens are actively devouring the plinths. Rocks are edible. For lichen, easily digestible. Some names are illegible, the dates no longer correspond to a linear timeline. This year there are many muskrat and possum babies, and they are very enthusiastic. They are healthy and nourished. They are bonding in the open cemetery plots.

All of it entangled. Everything mulched. We act on so little knowledge. The knowledge is already in our bones.

living here   Imagine!
would rather   it provides
an ominous
question
total fog   we
we
we   an atmosphere of
you don't resolve problems   you

impose them
potatoes
would arrive
always on time or,
no time
who can stop
blue sky
blue window
blue sky seen only through the blue window
these wrists
have only known how to be bound and unbound
there are no
refraction
closer to the body leave freedom
are you listening

? ? ?

The cemetery is home, and the potato field is home, and bodies within bodies are home. One body provides refuge for another within and outside themselves. Sometimes we get a glimmer of the magic of convolution and everything shimmers with crystalline rainbows; other times the sensation is muted. Some are suspicious of these openings in space when everything is tandem, prefer things in their usual recognizable individual places. Water will flow to the sea regardless of dams. Water will break up icebergs. Sun will burn through rubber. Sun will scorch the earth when there is no shelter. Finding the openings is translation work, registering the many in the many as myriad secretions of everything.

Mosquitos come out of their swampy birthplace and start looking for blood. They are ravenous. With their fine-pointed proboscises they insert into the flesh, they extract nutrition, elegantly sipping. Of any animal, mosquitos incur the greatest human death toll, followed by snakes. Both the mosquito and the snake are living their lives, and the sustenance they require has to be iron rich. Iron is a desired metal. Most animals and flora require iron. The mosquito creates a tiny buzzing sound; its vibration is like the wind on a leaf. They are fragile and vulnerable, mighty, and prolific. A tiny puddle of water can support a large colony of mosquitoes. They are beautiful with their slender wings and scintillating buzzing and their love of blood and their love of flying. They arose in an evolutionary dream of standing water. They dream with stagnant, rotting plants. When there is heat and mugginess, they thrive and show that a world can flourish in uncomfortable conditions. Mosquitos are a gathering force of zoonotic transfer. Bacteria from one animal makes its way into another through the mosquito's pointed member. The male mosquito pollinates flowers, the female sucks blood. Sharing bacteria from host to host, the female mosquito is a messenger. Killing the messenger poses its own risks.

There is a place for the mosquito in the ecosystem. The Earth requires their buzzing, which signifies an undertone of swamp, marsh, stagnant water. As descendants of the house fly, they morphed into tiny flying stingers, aggravating a feeling of peace and calm, killing as they populate.

Mosquitos gather along the edges of the salt marshes, laying their eggs in the floodwater, in small pools, along the outskirts of fields.

It will rain, says the wind. It will always rain eventually. When time stops for a moment, the mosquitos know that a spirit has crossed over from one realm to the other, from one world to another world; the gates deep in the forest open for those who have the keys to activate the portal. In those few seconds in which time is still, the mosquitos gather, lay their eggs, and go about their business, and when time snaps back, the mosquitos have gathered, have been working, have been in transition all along. The humans are always doing their best, (*I'm doing my best,* she keeps repeating to her son, *I'm doing my best*, he echoes to his partner), but not what is required. In the swamp there lies buried an old pick-up truck, several broken flowerpots, and what looks like the remains of helicopter propellers. The humans ask, *Where does the virus come from?* They always look outwards, to other species—to the mosquitos in the marshes, to the dead animals in foreign markets—as if species is a real designation, as if the mosquito isn't already an extension of the human, the human an extension of mosquito, the virus an extension of world, the world an extension of virus, the human as a virus, the human as assemblage, the human as marsh, the human as a broken flowerpot, the human as creator of words like "species," the human as the remains of helicopter propellers with nowhere left to go.

Emergent viruses and bacteria are being designed by the coordination of flora and fauna in relation to minerals—their fruiting/dying/birthing/shitting bodies and the decay of life passing into life. There is a virus that causes hallucinations. The hallucinations create a block from distinguishing one reality from another, as a hallucination is a reality in and of itself within all reality.

There is endless creativity of how bodies form and how bodies communicate. To know you is to become you and vice versa. We all are losing track of where we begin and end and whose dream we are dreaming and whose sorrow we are ingesting. The helicopter propellers were designed for a different stealth mission. Few are aware of the parameters of that mission. Few know the collateral damage. The body of the helicopter decomposes also. Metal rots, disintegrates. The earth is belching heavy metals and some of the metal of the propellers is from deep earth. In one hallucination, it seems that humans are in charge, and in an alternative hallucination, they have very little effective power. The hallucinations merge like water and oil and then submerge into the reality that supports all cognitive versions of life and death. There is no backup file for these versions. They are lived out and replicated, they are lived out and die off. Someone will have a dim remembrance of a possibility of one version. Others are quick to give labels to the versions. Naming something can result in instant death or longevity, it all depends. The swamp is a creative bastion of envisioning because transformation is readily active. For a world to form, there must be a hallucination and a reality and they must merge.

Swamp: The world is always at the juncture of an alternative beginning.

The Virus: The code is a beginning.

Granite: Minerals are a beginning.

Sky: Atmosphere is generative.

A hallucination: I don't see what you are talking about. Describe it again.

A hallucination: The deadliest creatures want to be human, but this isn't possible any longer.

An unnamed human: We want a reckoning so let's initiate a reckoning.

The State: Not so fast, citizens!

The Law: Stand down!

The Protest: We refuse!

[*The Police use pepper spray and sound cannons.*]

The Protestors: We defund the police, we dissolve the police.

The Virus: We will evolve together by a recipe of great purpose.

Mosquito: It was as if I was being attracted by a magnet. I glimpsed the pool of water and I had to get closer. Something drew me near, closer and closer.

Squirrel: In the distance there was a fire. I had to climb up higher and higher to see the flames. I could smell the damage, and I grieved. I grieved everyone who was burning and falling and unable to escape. I looked for the sacred tree but couldn't sense it anymore.

Tree: I felt the flames approach. Even before they were in the vicinity, I could feel shooting pain in my roots, in the mycelial networks tying us all together. Comrades being burnt alive in other parts of the forest, in other parts of the world.

Worm: It was immense. The dirt. The soil. We labored.

Seed: It was spellbinding to be carried away on the wind that the flames created. So close to death, so close to life. The edge itself as birth and creation. Remember us.

The Birds: We remember.

The Bees: Nibble, nibble.

Squirrel: I can still hear the howling, the howling and wailing all night long. For twenty-six days or more, the wailing. That's one measure of grief, the number of days spent wailing. But the hard part comes after that. Returning to life. Returning to presence. We all have to open up again and remember permeability. To stay hidden behind the walls upsets the flow.

Wolf: I used to howl all night. I was quite disturbed by everything I saw. I didn't want to leave. But they left me.

Seed: We ask the ocean for help.

Do you remember the rat who found the slice of pizza on a subway platform and began tugging at it until another rat came by and tried to wrest it from the first rat? That is not the story of Cain and Abel but the story of two rats bound by the city, trying to get a meal. Fast food is like that. You take a bite, and the meal drops into a moving train.

Older rat: Excellent slice—mushrooms and all.

Younger rat: Yes, nice slice. Move away or I'll wrestle you for it.

Older rat: Go ahead, I'm prepared for this fight.

Younger rat: Do you hear the oncoming train?

Older rat: Worse yet, I hear the spray of the exterminator.

Temporarily the subway is used by first responders only and no one is indulging in pizza on their commute. The pizza is a hallucination from a different era. Now in order to feed the family you have to drag food much further. It is arduous to drag food from street level into the subway tunnel, down steps, around corners, and out of view of the first responders who are more skittish than usual.

Older rat: I found a bagel and got it nearly to my warren when a human kicked it out of my grip.

Younger rat: I found it after it landed on the tiled surface—that bagel kept me alive.

Now is the time of food proliferation and food shortage. Many are growing gardens, and many are feeling the desert encroach on forests. A desert is a fast-moving entity. A desert is fast and furious and the sound of grains of sand is frightening. A desert works in monolithic expanses. Wind works in the desert's favor. Skin gets thicker. Eyelids become sealed. The desert is actively growing as a living entity. Anomalous in identity, the desert and the rat understand one another. Before the desert encroaches, there is a proliferation of poisonous toads. The state suggests that citizens catch them, put them in plastic bags, and freeze them for 48 hours. The toad's secretions instantly kill pets and small human children. Their populations are growing in huge proportions due to the increased temperatures and the lawns that humans water. The appearance of toads often signals epic change. The appearance of deserts signals epic, long-lasting change. Once topsoil is removed by the wind, seeds can't sprout. The toads foreshadow the desert, and the desert foreshadows the ocean.

In the desert, there are glistenings, reflective movements in shoes left out to dry, outside of camping tents, scurried movements that reflect moonlight to those watching. For a brief moment, all of the scorpions that have been hiding emerge from the darkness to reveal themselves, overfilling smelly shoes and boots left out on porches, creeping onto tents as the humans sleep, scampering over the plants and cacti and low trees to create new terrifying shapes, the silhouettes shapeshifting against the rising run.

In the large cities, there are rats spilling out of gutters, sewer openings, cracks in the wall. Sewer grates are thrust open, and the armies of rats come running out of subway stations. They fill subway cars when the doors slide open, humans screaming and running into each other trying to get out of the way. The rats create piles of bodies and use their momentum to overfill dumpsters, and when they are done with the dumpsters, they move inside into the kitchens of Michelin 3-starred restaurants, falling into pots of boiling soup and raiding pantries. All of the rats spill out into the streets, the rats in the streets enact a different kind of uprising and the humans don't know where to hide, don't know how to protect themselves.

In other cities, the squirrels all gather outside at once, romping on rooftops like loud neighbors upstairs, digging up seeds, and tunneling through carefully curated and maintained garden beds. The squirrels emerge from attics and basements and densely foliated trees and sneak into bedrooms, make nests out of expensive duvet covers and linen sheets, take over parks and playgrounds, parents screaming as their children try to pet the squirrels and keep them as pets.

All the havoc is prolific. Centipedes and millipedes join in on the ruckus. Everyone and everything from below ground comes to the surface. Watertight edifices succumb to saturation. Insects cry at their highest frequency. The din is alarming. The virus takes note of the upheaval. There is reorientation underway. Humans lose their categorical identity. To be human is not a fortified shell, it is a concept. The conceptual notion starts to melt or crawl away or is eaten away by snakes and groundhogs interested in different conceptual flavors. The ocean strips everything down to its origins. Out of the ocean come crabs and sea life not seen before on the shoreline. Shimmering translucent sea slugs who live at great depths come to the surface. Whales beach themselves, become immobile. Birds land on the whales' bloated bodies. There are seismic rumbles. The ground is unsteady. Humans have started to leave the cities in a panic. Cats and dogs run around hectically without their human companions. The trees are stripped bare of fruit and then of bark. It rains and there is lightning. Canned food is emptied out. Tin cans roll in the street. Garbage is everywhere. Weeds spring up. Roadways are choked up. Viruses come out of different sources. There are unending earthquakes. The tremors shake canyons and rock formations. Snakes come out of their holes. The rats take a break for a few days to sit it out. The ravens fly around to warn of impending disaster. The turtles know of the endless apocalypses on auto feedback, so they call it reality. Now comes the rain. Now comes the heat. Now comes the noisiness of everyone's voices. Someone cries for their doctor. Someone cries for their lawyer. Someone cries for their mother. The cries go unnoticed in the cluster of other noises. I know I was supposed to go to a doctor's appointment. The doctor's office is gone. Where are we? Yes, this is definitively Earth. Do you recognize your home? Do you know if this is the neighborhood where we congregate? Are these creature familiars all residents of the same neighborhood? Wasn't there a hospital here, a supermarket? Why is there a sticky substance flowing over the surface of the earth? Why does it feel simultaneously dry and also super-hot? Confusion. Unknowing. The feeling of wanting to opt out. The news has stopped. Information is coming from different channels. The internet is down. Wasn't there supposed to be an election? Wasn't there supposed to be a vaccine? We are past the period of belligerence. The crying means something else.

What's happened? / It's chaos, it's chaos I tell you. / We need to work together to rebuild. It's a collective effort. / Just keep a positive attitude and we'll get through it. / Jobs, what will we do about the lack of jobs? / What will our children do for money? / How will I get my prescriptions? / What about my coffee? / What do you mean I have to wait in line?

The complaints are numerous. The concerns, the words of advice, the instructions. The humans are concerned about getting things back to normal. They are concerned about the lack of jobs and the failing economy. They can't imagine that rebuilding could bring about something other than the same system that has already failed them. An anecdote tells of a man trapped in a room. His only access to the outside is a window that shows the blue sky outside. The man is asked to draw an image of freedom, and what he draws is the blue window. His vision of freedom is a replication of the architecture of his incarceration. The blue window is already and always a product of his circumstances of that system that keeps him imprisoned. So, escape is problematic. Escaping one's present circumstances might lead you back to the same circumstances. The humans scream and panic, *The world is ending!* and they plot their escape. They are also in that tiny room with the window to the blue sky. They flock to the window, tapping on the glass, pressing their faces against it while the room is in flames, while they are stung by hornets and swallowed by rats and the virus jumps from body to body—and in trying to protect themselves, they rip each other apart. No one wonders how the hornets, the rats, and the virus entered the room. No one understands the window as a window. No one wonders how small this room really is, and how vast the world outside might be. Yet. For now, this small room burns, the walls crumble into pieces, and yet the pile of corpses under the window has kept the window intact. All that remains is that window, sitting under a blue sky in the middle of the prairie, in the middle of an island, in the middle of space. It doesn't matter where the window is because a window is a window, and while we are still looking *through*, we are still on the other side.

I touch my greasy hair and unkempt body with my grubby hands and ask myself where I should wander when I know that I have to quarantine in place, as it is mandated to stay within the confines of one's home. Although we are free to wander anywhere, we can't be together, we can't touch. Touch is important. A depression falls over our social body. Instead of touching my creature familiars, I touch flora and fauna and mineral bodies fruiting and dissolving into the earth. The rockiness of my body becomes more pronounced. The statues of the originators of the system are falling; they are being dislodged from their bases. Symbols of violence are being stripped away. I touch the base of the former statue of a conquistador who somehow thought he found a new world. He and his travelers were outsiders. The bronze statue of his likeness is drowning in a river. Fish swim by. The nation-state relies on trade, but with borders closed, trade is at a standstill. People begin to make things for each other. Things are reused. Travel is not possible for most of the population—leisure travel, that is. Only a few planes fly overhead.

The wailing, my god, the wailing. It will not stop, and so neither, therefore, must I.

Inside, the small dog whimpers and shudders, trembling with fright. She frantically looks for somewhere to hide, under the nightstand, inside the shoe rack, the narrow corridor between the bathroom wall and the toilet. Nowhere is it *safe*. Nowhere is there actual refuge. The woman tries to comfort the dog. The woman is frustrated by the dog's inability to be comforted, is disgusted by the dog's proximity to the uncleaned toilet, picks up the dog and brings her to bed.

Outside, fireworks go off and the dog bites in response. A bite lands on the woman's middle finger and she yelps out in pain. She picks up the dog and sets her down on the bed, cursing and yelping. The blood spills out over the bathroom counter, and outside, there are still fireworks going off, there is still the valence of war and outcry and celebration. What is the gesture of celebration with the sound that also signals the harbinger of death? Why an explosion to signal joy? Whose joy? Whose celebration? Whose power over whom? Again and again. The dog doesn't understand the *politics* of such gestures, nor the history of why these upsetting sounds exist. But that doesn't make the dog any more ignorant of what is happening, of what the sounds really mean.

Does the soul reside in the pineal gland or is it dispersed among organs and systems within the body? The juvenile squirrels still sip from their mother's nipple and clamor around in the trees, trying to identify sources of food, all new, yet not alienating—for a squirrel it is normal to think of verdant young buds as nourishment. The space above their eyes buzzes with fireworks—the sky's crackling has been relentless. They don't know of a time before the sounds of violent bursting air stirring psychic forces. The pituitary gland blends with the pineal gland and forms a triangulation with the eyes. Seeing becomes immersive with the soul. There is a crown above the formation and it looks out with its jeweled perspective. It can see the crowds, the uprising—the fifteen-thousand people gathered to honor the lives of black trans women, all wearing white, waving, and swaying with the closeness, contact, allyship. The pituitary connects to the spine. Each vertebrae communicates messages up the brainstem. Two young lawyers are arraigned for hurling a Molotov cocktail into a police vehicle that had been previously destroyed by other protestors. Someone takes a cell phone photo of them and shares it with the police. They enter the carceral system that they so ardently fought against. Both young lawyers have been advocates of the poor, of those who aren't granted representation. They are torn from the social world of movement and being in the world and are placed into a system of lockdown and fright. The systems are codependent. The social world of movement and being is also a system of fright and constriction. A prime feature of the society is its enterprise around prisons—the prison-industrial system. The money that is made by incarceration can't be underestimated. The prison does the heavy lifting of maintaining the system of inequity.

The energies of the spine congeal around the midsection of the chest. There is heaviness and there is trouble breathing.

The crisis focuses on the destruction, on the damage done. Property has been destroyed. This cannot go unpunished. What is deserved? What is justice? What is earned, not earned? The ends or the means? Responding to the crisis with the energy of the crisis replicates the crisis and the citizens find themselves in a loop. There is a relationship between weeding and protest. There is a relationship between death and the sky. There is a relationship between a dandelion seed and that feeling of your chest being torn open, that it's just too difficult to go on, that the despair is just too much and this broken heart of yours will never mend because it's all too much. There is a relationship between overwhelm and the moss growing on the leaking drainpipe on the side of the house. There is a relationship between breath and no breath.

Still, the dust swirls in the wind and reminds us where we came from. Still, we might peer over the edge into the abyss and remember that we are still here and there is a long way yet to fall. When the woman rides her bike to the store to buy eggs, she notices the squirrels running around and chasing each other around tree trunks, across streets, lawns, and gardens. The squirrels are still chasing lovers, are still giving in to the seasonal cycles, and their own urges and desires. The woman wears gloves and a mask and in her purse is a bottle of hand sanitizer and a small knife. These are the tools of the revolution, she thinks. *This is how we will instigate change*, she thinks. She doesn't hear what the squirrels are saying, doesn't see past the asphalt immediately in her purview, doesn't see the sky opening up above her, the sky's chest being torn open, the beams of light radiating downward from the sky's own broken heart.

The virus too is on the rise. The uprising is getting perpetually stronger, as is the virus. Many states that hadn't experienced much infection early on are seeing a spike in contagion. Not only elderly members of the society—young people also are being impacted by the illness. The protests so far have not been identified as a spreader of the virus. Bars, restaurants, places of worship, and hair salons have. Nursing homes, meatpacking plants, and prisons are experiencing menacing outbreaks. The virus is now an ever-present global hum of reality. The protests hum the truth about social justice in the face of utter disparity and violence. Humans are forming alliances by coming out to the rallies, letting their fear slip away, joining the crowds, feeling the power of transformation. The fire of change is registered by the pineal gland. There is a hum and a glow where there are great crowds. The rallies bring strength in numbers and an immunity to fear. The ocean is warming and feeling restless also. There is a formative force, etheric in nature, that travels below the surface of appearance. Worms, insects—swarming, amassing, burrowing. Great white sharks are coming close to the shore. Dorsal fins sticking out above the waterline indicate arrival.

The uprising is the movement of the ocean tides, water as water, the permeable and expansive nature of bodies. The uprising is the song the marchers sing as they advance down the street, fists in the air, singing in unison, thousands of voices that reverberate between the buildings, the sound waves penetrating the foundations of old buildings ready to be demolished. The uprising is every emotion blown open, the sky releasing its own haunted loneliness onto the ground below, the archetypal blue that resonates with the frequency of ancient love, of future compost, the memory of a future that will hold our grief that is ordinary and necessary. Don't worry, we've all died a million times and will die a million times more. It's not death that is to be feared, nor life. The trembling, the shuddering, the fear of living with pain, rather than dying without it. The co-dependencies that bind us together. What else can we release when we rise from our graves once again?

Police cars can be endlessly manufactured but they are obsolete, as is the paradigm of policing. Their obsolescence creates violent rage in those unwilling to accept the change of calibration. Police cars, like statues of confederate leaders, are relics and as such are being dismantled. The rage of those who want to prevent these actions can be heard crossing the blood-brain barrier. When the paradigm shifts, the noise is always high decibel. A reign of terror is replaced by community management. Investing in infrastructures of care changes the streets. A future rises up. The imagining of this future travels through the spinal cord into the ocean toward mountains, into lakes. The tyrants run for cover. They've built bunkers for themselves and have plenty of supplies. This might be the way that the visible and invisible world meet. The way that the individual and the collective cohere into magic reversal. Revolutionary dreams well up. There is incredible energy within the collective. Each strand mutates and becomes stronger, more resilient, more committed. There is a predominance of warmth. People find their telepathic abilities restored. People ask each other what they need and share abundantly. No one cares to hold onto an excess of anything material or psychic. Electrical in nature, snakes are attracted to changes in energetic patterns. A black snake regurgitates the oil stored in her belly. Oil pours over the fields.

When the invisible is made visible, the words come out of my mouth like flailing arms, and the flailing branches of trees resemble sentences. Obviously, I've lost something. Obviously, I've learned to see something else. There is the habit of asking others to do everything for us, and when we see ourselves as independent, it's a performance of the individual. It is time for bed, and I ask out loud, "Can I have a glass of wine?" No one in particular responds. No one in particular gives me permission. The words collide in the space around my body and make a heavy noise and I wonder about the room I'm in. I can't tell yet that it is morning, and not night, and I've already gone to bed, but I don't remember because the dream I had became the reality I lived today, and real life has become more fantastical than the mundanity of my dream life in the transferal. There is a sentence, there, in the space in front of me, but I can't grasp the syntax and I want to ask, "What are you saying? What are you trying to say to me?" But I don't even know who the "you" is, and it is obvious still that I've lost something, but I had told myself that I wouldn't think about these kinds of things in terms of loss or gain, and I think to myself, *I just need some water, I just need some water.* I can't remember anymore but the energy of the sentence tells me to stand upright, to stay standing, to stay rooted. "Ok," I say out loud, to no one in particular. "Ok."

"Ok" is an affirmative utterance that echoes around the universe. Once "ok" is released, it sets off a chain reaction. "Ok" is like "go." They aren't equivalent statements, yet they eventuate similar mechanisms of release. Water. Water running through a public system. Water from the sky, the clouds, the lake. Abundant water. A metaphor that engages water as its epicenter. Water for survival. Water for dreaming and dream life. One simple glass of water to get through the night of unknown dispositions and visions. I found my way to the kitchen and ran the faucet and filled a glass and then another member of my family came toward me, evidently also needing a glass of water. We communed around water and its meanings. We decided to bike to the lake and release our feelings, feelings that had multiplied without our realization. It became ok to let things go—let go of things. The sun came up as we stood there mesmerized by our feelings. The release created a torrent. In my right hand was a large reddish spider. The spider released itself into the air. I saw a snake with her eggs. I saw multiple chipmunks with seeds in their mouths. The rain came down and it felt wonderful. I understood somewhat what a floral member of my family feels like in the rain shower. This form of awareness felt slippery and warm. The water felt warm. The lake felt warm. Lakes are organs of existence. I didn't have a fever. The atmosphere was tepid. I was absorbing a totality of togetherness. Life in its myriad forms was creating moisture on her upper lip.

Spider with a red hourglass mark under its belly: Ok.

Rain drizzle: Ok.

Chipmunk, with a missing ear: Ok.

Chipmunk, his brother: Ok.

Green garden snake: Ok.

Water: Ok.

Virus: Ok.

Grapefruit seed: Ok.

Motor oil: Ok.

Sky: Ok.

Tree, growing in a city: Ok.

Ashes: Ok.

A woman who is also a teacher who thinks of herself as a spiritual leader of sorts sneezes in her garden and then hurries inside. The pollen count is too high today. This woman is allergic to everything. The permeability of her body has gone awry and the only solution she sees is to barricade herself at home and eat a strict diet of pre-approved foods. As her condition worsens, and as she is impacted more and more by outside influences, foods, microbes, she makes stricter and more stringent rules to regulate her living patterns. This is a survival story. This is the fault of the world and its processed foods and pollution and the virus. She knows best how to keep herself alive. Her world gets smaller and smaller as she reaches out from her cave to keep her relationships intact. Everyone needs to engage with her according to her rules. She is open to critique, she tells her students, but her students don't want to explain their life stories, and in order to explain why one gesture might not be the best one, the context required is centuries of history. So, the students who might have something to say remain silent. This is not a safe place for them to be open. So, the students who should remain silent have much to say. For them, every space should be safe and the more they speak, the more they believe that they are making progress in their spiritual growth. "Ok?" asks the teacher. "Ok," the students respond.

When every presence conspires to become a noxious source of discomfort, there is a feeling of overwhelm and retreat. Things that shouldn't be detrimental prove to be poisonous or cause harm. She retreats and finds no solace. She forms aversions. Her body freezes up. She feels stiff to the point of paralysis. Some mornings, only with extreme will is she able to endeavor to move. The feeling is of being out of recognition with herself and the world. She has become estranged from herself and others. She knows that she can't escape the presence of the world. Her allergies are indicative of something psychic as well as material-physical, but she can't pinpoint what the sources are. She has subverted whatever lurks under her psyche. She succumbs to the suffering but resists opening up to the relief. Her students look to her as a role model. They also harbor feelings of shame and abandon. She is emblematic of dissolution. The students who need her become sullen, silent. The ones who are brazen and think they know what they need to know become tyrannical, arrogant. The class has become one of oppositional energy. All of this is symptomatic. She needs to recalibrate around the elements. She needs a new alliance with the world. She needs to revert to unknowing and search for an opening. She needs to start somewhere else and rebuild confidence with her body's relationship to presence. If the world is toxic, she has to identify the toxicity as present, not hide from it. Can she live with the toxins and suffer? Because it is becoming impossible to shelter or quarantine from toxicity. The toxicity she experiences as an assault is invisible, textureless, unapparent. Blood tests reveal her body's revolt. She decides to visit an old friend who is also somewhat of a spiritual teacher to see what they have to say about her predicament. She is desperate; she can't go on in this state alone.

In the forest outside the city, lightning strikes a tree in the middle of the night. The tree is dry and brittle and shoots up in flames. The flames jump from the tree to the dry brush in the surrounding area, to the other trees nearby, the flames growing and expanding and consuming what they find in their path. The fire is lively and fierce. It did not even exist a few minutes ago, and currently it is large and fearsome. Nearby animals sense the danger and scatter. Those who are able to, run away. In one hollowed-out tree near the fire, a squirrel sleeps soundly, doesn't hear the screams and doesn't smell the smoke. The fire creeps up the trunk and the smoke permeates the bark, filling the hollow space in which the squirrel sleeps. The squirrel never wakes, the smoke permeates his dreams, lulls him into a deeper and deeper sleep, takes him on another journey into the sky. In the morning, when the fire has died down and all that is left is charred bones and ashes where the squirrel once slept, he has already made his way into another realm.

Her house also succumbs to the flames. She slept the night on her sofa and didn't awaken to the crackling of fire—she had taken a few sleeping pills to ease her into sleep. Her students received word the following day. They were dazed and speechless. All decided unanimously to host a memorial. Everyone came together to remember her. Her house was burnt to the ground. It was an old house made of wood and had burned quickly. She was an apparition and a memory. Everyone said they didn't really know her. No one knew her age or where her family lived. No one knew where she grew up, or when she had moved to the town. Her garden was intact—many vegetables to be harvested on the vine. Fruit trees, herbs. She didn't have a partner. She had cleared her hard drive recently. There was very little evidence of her existence remaining. There was ash among the timbers. Her teeth didn't burn. A ring she wore was located under the mattress springs of the sofa. A downpour washed the ash away. There was no burial and no marker, and her body was scattered by the rain and the wind. Her students talked about her frequently. They psychoanalyzed who she was, what they knew of her.

The light coming in through her green curtains had comforted her on many mornings, that strange eerie but bright glow that permeated her space, reminding her of the outside and the warmth, but unable to participate fully in that resonance. The curtains had burned, as had the window, though the light remained, and the light was already everywhere. The wind blows the ashes and scatters them with the dandelion seeds, and where there is death, there is always already life. What does the uprising look like after everything has burned down? When does the uprising end and when does it begin again? Who will be there to rise when the entire world is in ashes? All of the dead will be there. All of them.

DARKNESS

Darkness is the absence of light. Or darkness is not necessarily the absence of light, rather a fullness of ambiance that glows. Darkness can contain multitudes. During darkness, there is night. During darkness, there is fear, and during fear, there is a kind of reckoning in that damp chill running up one's spine.

The city streets are no longer kept clean of debris by municipal street sweepers. Seeds collect in cracks and crevices. Within months, stands of weeds have responded to the early summer rain and proliferated. Their foliage creates shade that allows for an understory of life to flourish. The city transforms into a meadow. The same ruderal species that cling to mounds of rubble at abandoned construction sites are the ones that root themselves on pedestrian walkways and major avenues of transportation. Most of these plants have powerful medicine. They are opportunistic. They understand renewal.

Mugwort is one of the first settlers to grip into the dirty micro-canyons of the sidewalk. Frilly and almost velvety, its leaves are aromatic. Any person who rubs up against a mugwort of the *Artemisia* genus will carry intense perfume with them. Plants understand disturbance. The first to arrive are hardy—require little water, can tolerate harsh conditions. They create an emergent environment for the more sensitive flora to follow. Mugwort is celebrated for relieving malaise, ameliorating stomach and intestinal conditions, helping with irregular menstruation, and healing scarring. Since the Iron Age, mugwort has been used as a flavoring, especially in ale, and also in many culinary dishes.

In the blazing light of disruption, mugwort begins an architecture of shadow. Shadow is a conduit for moisture, the medium of growth. With tall, stalky growth, its spiky leaves create jagged shade. Mugwort anticipates disaster, converts it from an event to a changeable condition.

Ruderal plants demonstrate what liberation looks like. They live a sense of possibility in a space that is failing, faltering. Together with mugwort, Queen Anne's lace often exists in the slim fissures of concrete and asphalt busted open by the elements. They are able to share micro-spaces and yet defy a sense of crowdedness. The plants form a momentarily *we*, a symbiotic collectivity that is mediated by weather, brought about by displacement. Queen Anne's lace is also edible, of the carrot family. Milk thistle joins—is edible; yellow dock grow alongside, also edible. Yellow dock contains chemical components that kill parasites, bacteria, and fungi. A curative for sexually transmitted diseases and an aid for pain and swelling. Alongside them are chickweed, creeping Charlie, chicory, yellow sweet clover, and daisy fleabane—all edible. What is notable is that most weeds are edible, medicinal, and herbal; compared with ornamental plants often arranged symmetrically in formations of human design—these tend to be poisonous and not sustainable for anyone.

Rainbow attends to a garden of catnip. The plants offer themselves up for tasting, rubbing, and sniffing. Such ecstasy is conveyed. Rainbow tunes into the frequencies. He chirps alongside the plants. The garden is a nurturing and healing apex. Rainbow, in his seventeenth year, is an elderly cat. He is sustained by herbs and the sun. Every year the plants grow more profusely. Rainbow revels in garden life. He is sustained by field mice and his passion for trees. His friendship with squirrels is an important component of his social life. All day when he isn't napping, he convenes with squirrels. They are part of his extended family. When night descends, he flourishes. Many other animals are resting; he is out roaming, sometimes getting into combat with other tomcats. The sun has set, and he makes his way around his stomping grounds, noticing every tree, bush, and rock, checking for scents—a delivery of information. He will bring this information into his body, into his home. This coexistence is an interspecies arrangement. Like the sun and the moon, Rainbow moves in spheres of relation. He uses mental telepathy to communicate with presences other than himself. Images move through the forcefield and rematerialize in the minds of those he projects to.

Darkness is the twin of the sun—of star formations, a reverse-positive energy necessary to relieve excess radiation, excess concentration on outline and shape. Darkness is what we come out of and into during phase changes. In the forest, *Armillaria ostoyae* revels in the rich darkness of soil and roots. They have been personing the woods for two thousand four hundred years and their bodies cable underground some three and a half miles. A biography of this person would take many moons to disclose—in a radically egalitarian unraveling. They are consanguineous in a realm of the consanguine. Each extension, an expository device composing the daylight, composing the darkness.

When you take something from somewhere, you might drop it,

you might forfeit holding the object. The object falls or the object morphs or the object eats you alive. As it should be. Possession begs the question of how we can be together. With our rhizomorphs we reach out to you.

What is the work of darkness if not the persistence of presence. Not exclusive of light, a counter-brilliance, to forever be holding, to forever be everywhere, holding each and every crack and crevice, each dark expanse ready to be revealed, this is the work of darkness, to allow oneself to be welcomed and made over, to allow oneself to work in the shadow and see what was previously unseen come into the light so that wounds can be held by love too, the labor of darkness, the labor of light, the labor of silence, the labor of words. Oh! The labor of earthworms.

A squirrel emerges from the thick foliage; scraping paw sounds on the bark. The sun has not risen yet, but one wouldn't necessarily describe it as "dark" outside. It is a beckoning, a portal, the darkness lifting. But then again, hasn't the darkness been lifting all along? Our eyes, perhaps, just weren't attuned to detect the subtle transition.

The cat convenes with the squirrels—juveniles and adults all gather for seeds in the morning. The cat has sat with the squirrels for many years this way. He licks his hind legs, bites his tail repeatedly to clean his fur. He dreams of the jaguar and the jaguar dreams of him. They have never met: cat and jaguar. The squirrels and the cat dream together and hold the space of the garden. Insects fly through the garden. Bees hover around the squirrels and the cat. The soil is teaming with microorganisms actively building their world. Banana peels are decomposing in the soil and the salad greens are interesting to the hornets. The garden world intersects with the city world by being always here within but also by holding a space that is quite different. The squirrel elder that died several months ago is completely gone. Her bones were chewed up by another member of this garden community. The jaguar goes about eating their prey by eating the eyes first. Prey. Has the lettuce been preyed upon? Now is the time for a conceptual change, and the language to make it happen could be uncovered in the soil, in the garden, from the cats, from the squirrels. The summer is hot and that heat revolutionizes the climate.

Even tied down, the tomato plants can reach for anything.

The dandelion seeds are still and already a reminder of every journey one must go through.

When the squirrel wipes his paws in the dirt, he spreads the dandelion seeds, the moss spores, the soil; the entanglement of particles is also the climate, the mixture of breath and air.

The cat breathes in, the insects buzzing and flying around the flower buds. The cat breathes out, the soil yet teeming, the soil yet building, being built, being and becoming already and always.

The squirrel breathes in and the tomato plant breathes out. The squirrel breathes out and the moss breathes in.

Who remembers the flicker of the flame before the darkness settled down to keep us warm?

Who remembers the bright lights above that held the distance at bay, that kept distance like keeping time on a watch?

Who remembers what it was like, when everything was lit and translucent, and we could see each other, see through each other, as clearly as we see each other now?

The heat is intense. The heat is particularly intense at the poles. Ice many millennia thick is melting and what is uncovered is darkness—a core of darkness that merges with the darkness of the oceans. The darkness of the squirrel's memory has converged with the cat's pineal gland secretions. The Milky Way is an aura that is a form of darkness pulsating with light. Now that the heat is upon us, we become sluggish and listless or agitated and violent. An itchiness pervades. Did she rub against a poisonous plant? How is the body adapting to the increase in heat? Heartbeats are more pronounced. The desert is expanding and, with it, vocabulary is shrinking. Is this true? The opposite is also possible, language could be expanding to describe the conditions of its emergence. Language is a special kind of translucency—one can look into and through objects and concepts with language and also enforce an opacity that is self-reflective, or deflective, and means something besides its literal interpretation. The darkness is a form of vibrancy that language rejoices in. Now is the time to develop a proficiency in soil's ability to shelter micro-reality within itself. The creation and production of soil is the creation and production of sky—worlds not held down by gravity. Turn your gaze to the synecdoche of soil because a cosmological understanding requires this.

Air fills the squirrel's lungs and organizes itself in the space that it finds itself in, the lungs feel both full and idle and the squirrel runs around the perimeter of the tree in an effort to meet his mate. He has given himself the task of *this mate* and so has set certain expectations for himself that he may or may not meet, but these tasks are not written down in any planner or agenda so they may change at any time. This doesn't mean failure though, that's a capitalist term. And nor, of course, is this a task, but just a desire in the present moment that he will follow until it doesn't make sense to follow anymore. When describing the actions of the squirrel, human language is inadequate. We mimic the organizational structures from our own corporate reality and forget how language warps everything we see, how colonial these sentences really are. As if there is a *supposed to* or *should*. As if there is a *cause* and *effect*. As if time is linear. As if we understand anything we are seeing. As if we understand anything at all.

Rhythm has been colonized, as have the definitions of how to describe and conceive of worlds within worlds. This particular language demands crisp neat sentences. Legibility means abiding by the semantical portent of the rules. Sentences hold the meaning in place, like all confinement structures there is violence that makes this happen. Otherwise, meanings would drift and roam, regroup, make love, disperse. Meaning doesn't care about sitting in place legibly. Meaning is the first to leave the room. Meaning is a mirage. Meaning would prefer to ramble in the open meadow or swim in the liquid of the jaguar's eyeball or fall from a tree landing on its furry tail. Meaning drizzles and bleeds and there isn't definition per say. A yelp can hold authentic meaning perhaps more than a human sentence. But the comparison is a farce. The sentences collapse upon themselves, and the collapse signals an opening. Suddenly there is a hole to burrow into, an opening! Scramble down the hole while you can. Open up to the core of the earth, the core of earthly existence. The confusion is the insight. Meanings require both darkness and light—legibility and shape as well as holistic solidity and oneness. The squirrels prefer to speak quietly in a vibratory manner. A low-decibel chatter. The sky speaks in thunder and lightning. Rubbing, as in friction, is a form of communication amongst persons in an ecosystem. Individual raindrops join the ocean currents and rub molecularly in a liquid overload of weight and tension. A yelp is oceanic and when you chew your tail you construct a sentence. Meanings stick together in clusters. Meanings repeal.

All of the yelps and howls and utterances and muddy, muddy sounds emanating from the bowels, the darknesses, the bellies, the pits.

p-p-p-i-t
f-f-a-f-a-f-f-a-a-f
e-e-e-e-g-h-e-e-s-h-k
s-s-s-s-s-s-s-s-s-h-h-h

c-o-n-t-r-o-l-l-l-l-l-l-l-e-d-d
l-o-o-o-o-o-s-h-h-h-o-o-o-o-o-w-g-k-j-h-r-b-v-a-z-x-h-k-j-e-v-c-a-s-q-z-z-z-z-z
b-o-o-s-h-b-o-o-s-h-b-b-b-o-o-o-o-s-s-h-h-h-h-h
! ?

His hand on my knee. My hand on his leg. Our hands brush up against each other. That electricity from the friction of hands, from the space in between, from the distance between hands that closes and opens again. The feeling of being suspended and then thrown down again. The shapes in the darkness that only call out when you are not listening.

Who is talking? Who is that? *Hello? Hello? Hello?*

Hello!

The sentence is magical because it strings together differences in a chain of effects. A spell is cast. The spell can last centuries. The sentence can be etched in rock. A string of words can hover as cloud formation spewed from an engine. The wind arranges words. The water changes the syntax of rocks, ancient braille. A sentence can accomplish liberation. With certain words sentences are reduced. Sentences are commuted—there is a pardon, release. With certain words a pipeline can be stopped in its tracks. The water protectors rejoiced when the courts declared that the pipeline would have to be emptied out and that a review of its feasibility would have to take place. Words shouted in the air, words written, words translated. The pipeline has been shut down. The black snake is laid to rest. Words could reactivate the snake or kill it altogether. Words contain a magic both lethal and healing at once. The sentence can cure the words and the words can cure the sentence. His anus looks like a spring flower, and with it in my face, he helps me understand his mood. Fur is a meaning, as is skin. We learn this the hard way oftentimes. The rocks speak with mineral action.

It's a slow-moving fire and it's the sky in its entirety. It's a pink nose aimed at the sun and the sneeze that revolves around uncertainty. It's all of the fires and an adjustment of faith, an adjustment of the towel, of one's hair clinging to a sweaty cheek, it's that sound he makes when he's asleep and makes your heart flutter because you know he's finally resting. It's that shrug of *who even knows anymore* and it's the door rattling on its hinge. It's nothing apparent. It's everything obvious. It's so empty. It's the removal of faith or rain or love or time.

Who are you? screams the sentence. There is no response.

After the fires there is an epic increase in domestic violence. Stress traveled from the flames to the tips of fingers, from carbon dioxide, water vapor, nitrogen, and oxygen to the lungs of humans who yell in distress. Thermite reactions agitate the hypothalamus. The women report that they no longer recognize their partners. Their actions don't make sense. Their emotions no longer correspond to the relationships at hand. The destruction caused by the fires has injected them with fury. Beatings, rapes, and risky behavior proliferate. Alter egos emerge from the shadows.

They've shed their lower limbs to resist fire. They've deposited their needles to suppress grasses from growing near their trunks. The fire is colossal. It doesn't heed precautions of a human scale.

The entire foliage is singed. The few remaining leaves fall off of the ash-encrusted tree trunks of those that stand. The trees are entirely denuded. Some seeds were buried under the burning embers. Lay in wait. One generation of deciduous and coniferous trees succumbs to the fury of the inferno. The heat of the fire melts the ground. The darkness of forests gives way to the stark-naked light of burnout. An epic event of tree mortality. Ponderosa pines, Douglas firs, quaking aspens, sugar pines: one-hundred-forty-nine million tree deaths in a single destructive incineration. The hummingbird, the grey catbird, their homes are reduced to rubble.

Darkness provides shelter, calm. A place to blend in. A sanctuary. Darkness grows in shade. Darkness is outside the visual spectrum, so it is a place of dreams. The forest needs to regrow to allow for dreams to flourish. This is a gray time of ash. Rock into dust and liquid body into ash. A dream dies with the caress and travels to the underworld with the tug of gravity and eventual rain. The deeper the dream travels, the more members of the underworld it encounters. The ancient gods of the underworld reside under the soil in recesses in the rock. Their contempt for human greed is immense. They show their rage and dismay by cannibalizing emotions.

Darkness calls the outer universe to itself, embracing the everything that exists together with everything that will become, intimacy is established. Space, infinitely expanding, then shrinks infinitesimally within molecules of non-luminous material for a microsecond. Hot dark matter incessantly wants to move, to relocate. Gravity is a muscle that holds the forces together as they bulge into a greater unknown. Neutron stars and black holes are the coming-together of future residences.

In my lower limbs is a singed koala infant who lost her mother. She quivers in the harsh light as I stand straight, harboring a resolve to stand straight. She embraces my trunk where the fires have scarred me. My bark is gone, her fur is gone. We mourn our situation together. She digs her burnt claws into me, I tear the sandy ground with my roots. I've stood here for one hundred cycles of the earth's revolution around the sun. All my mothers and fathers have also lived here. We've also blown in the wind elsewhere, in a circumference of familiarity. Sentience is a labyrinth. I grew to encounter the demeanor of homo sapiens. A frazzled woman rushes into the once-forest and notices the koala. She swaddles the stricken baby in her arms and heads back to her partially incinerated structure, once a house. She brings the koala to a rescue animal hospital. They give the koala oxygen and an intravenous drip to restore hydration. Grief can look like care. Care can look like grief. Mine is a steady death. I slowly evaporate without my bark to hold moisture in.

During the time of the virus and the time of the fires, the cutting down of vast swaths of forests continues. Forests succumb to the chainsaw and the paradigm of extraction capital. Cutting down the forests forces novel intimate contact between human and the other-than-human people who have lived for millennia in the sheltering habitat of dense woods and forest. The wild is a description of the uncapitalized. A mass exodus of animals ensues. Refugee status of microbes, pathogens—everyone looking for a home.

During the time of the virus there is a surge of gun violence in cities across the nation. It starts with randomized killings in broad daylight that take the form of drive-by shootings and nameless executions. Young children succumb to gunshot wounds.

The State's approach to quelling civil outrage metastasizes. Unmarked vans arrive with soldiers in unmarked camouflage outfits yielding automatic weapons and other devices of destruction, forcefully seizing protestors without due process, giving no indication of why the protestors are being hauled away and detained. The protestors continually gather and continue protesting, day after day, night after night, armed with homemade shields, leaf blowers, drums, and umbrellas. They hold hands and link arms. The protestors refuse to succumb to police scare tactics. One protestor's skull is shattered by a rubber bullet, others are maimed.

The State decides to reinstate killing inmates. Chemicals are prepared to be fed intravenously into perpetrator-victims. Added to the approved chemical toxins lethally injected are the options to use poison gas, firing squads, and electrocution. Waiting on death row is interminable, until it isn't.

Everyone is raw—unnerved. Derangement follows ecstatic indignation. People stumble and then strike out. The virus is detected in unborn fetuses. Smoke and ash from the fires exacerbate the virus' grip on bodies, on health outcomes.

A squirrel is diagnosed with bubonic plague. A young girl is mauled by a mountain lion, dolphins with stab and gunshot wounds wash ashore. An elderly woman, gored by a bison when she approached too closely in hopes of taking a selfie, is in critical condition at an unnamed hospital. Broken heart syndrome is on the rise.

The fire manifests light in its quest to consume fuel—its ultimate role, however, is to create darkness. White supremacy, a system that relies on inequality, extraction, and death metabolizes itself, as the rage it attempts to suppress rises up against it as a deluge, as a fire, as a fuel. The seeds are still scattering, still gathering, still wandering, still being incinerated.

Darkness was never the absence of light, as here it penetrates. Do you remember what it was like before the flashes began, when you could still close your eyes and not see the constant flashes and pangs? I feel it still surging in my bowels. I feel the electricity in my hands, and I want to dream it all again.

To be darkly present and also shining becomes the criteria for survival and justice.

This one's for you. For all of us.

Notes:

p. 39: Sara Ahmed, "Interview with Judith Butler," *Sexualities* 19, no. 4 (2016): 482–492.

p. 48: *Eros ton adynaton*, ('love of the impossible'), "a paraphrase of something said by Heracles' father Amphitryon in Euripides' *Heracles*. Neil Bartlett, *Oscar Wilde, In Praise of Disobedience*. (London, Brooklyn: Verso, 2020):146.

p. 56-57: Greta Thunberg's address to world leaders at the U.N.'s Climate Action Summit in New York. "How Dare You! Greta Thunberg Slams World's Focus on Economic 'Fairy Tales' While Ecosystems Collapse" *Democracy Now*, September 24, 2019, video and transcript, 4:42
https://www.democracynow.org/2019/9/24/un_climate_action_summit_greta_thunberg.

p. 58-59 Chief Raoni Metuktire, "Meet Brazil's Indigenous Leader Attacked by Bolsonaro at U.N. over Efforts to Preserve the Amazon," Interview by Nermeen Shaikh, *Democracy Now*, September 24, 2019, video and transcript, 5:00 https://www.democracynow.org/2019/9/24/un_climate_summit_indigenous_leader_barred.

p. 61: adrienne maree brown, *Emergent Strategy: Shaping Change, Changing Worlds* (Chico: AK Press, 2017): 34. (p. 61)

References to "the second body" owe a lot to a reading of Daisy Hildyard's book, *The Second Body*, Fitzcarraldo Editions (August 7, 2018)

Acknowledgements

Gratitude for all of the flora: especially the bald cypress tree, the dandelions, the artichoke, the sage bush.

Gratitude for all of the fauna: especially the squirrels, the crows, the geese, beloved animal companions in this realm and others (Benny, Maggie, Piper, Rainbow, Mumes, Tina, and Topaz...)

Gratitude for all of the mineral beings, the mountains, the elements, the sky, the oceans, the funga & vast mycelial network, beings that circumvent taxonomy, refuse categorization, show us how to transform and also ground ourselves in various forms, the ancient ones.

Gratitude even for the being known as the novel coronavirus, in all of its direct and elusive variations through time and space.

Gratitude for many humans, for their friendship, provocation, intimacy, and care, for their support and for everything we have learned: especially Toshi Iijima, Geoff Olsen, Laura Woltag, Megan Kaminski, Sophie Strand, Bayo Akomolafe, Petra Kuppers, Lidia Yuknavitch, Christine Shan Shan Hou. Generative, collaborative vibes abound!

The deepest thanks to the dearest humans of Meekling Press. We are lucky to be ensconced in total care and generosity.

This book represents the exuberance of friendship and what can happen when two symbiotic beings interlace their consciousness in language.

We were roommates at The Association for the Study of Literature and Environment conference (ASLE) that took place from June 26–30, 2019, at the University of California, Davis. The conference theme was "Paradise on Fire," a title so flagrant and apt as much of the planet was in the throes of unprecedented conflagration. Janice presented a paper, "Co-Dependencies & Becoming: The Language of Personhood," and Brenda presented a paper, "A Whole Cloud of Witnesses: Solastalgia in a Time of Environmental Emergency," just to give you a sense of what was already being breathed together. Together we sat in on numerous compelling talks that presented the vast, complex arena of thinking about Earth at a time of major transition and of Earth's sentience in its manifold significance. The conference inspired an interest in collaborating on an undisclosed project. With no planned agenda we began to make entries in a notebook we passed back and forth throughout the conference. We were guided by the previous entry one of us made, taking turns writing as we continued to participate in the osmosis of everything that surrounded us. We wrote entries during panels and also when finding a place to pause and rest within the huge campus garden. We made sure to pay close attention to the many diverse beings that lived within the university grounds and those that were visitors. The campus felt like a town created for floral beings.

Afterward, once the conference was over and Janice returned to Portland (OR) and Brenda to Brooklyn (NY), we resumed our writing over Zoom with an open Google doc. Though a contrast to the tactile, somatic, impressionistic experience of total immersion that we experienced, this different phase presented compelling changes in our modality. We entered into a veritable hypnotic state every time we met virtually to write. Responsiveness to the unfolding of actuality was what the process required. Portals into and out of conundrums presented themselves. Contradictions (if that's what they are) did not trouble us. Repetitions only proved that experiences rely on recurrence in difference. Actively, we navigated a coming-together in real-time to present stimuli as an offering. We didn't meta-cognate before or after writing. Questioning what we were making didn't occur. There was a powerful acceptance and nonattachment that entered our modality. What we chronicled became prismatic instantly: Prismatic in its attention to interspecies relations. Prismatic within time. Prismatic within space. Sometimes we smeared description, sometimes we mottled the architecture of narration so that an unraveling could be observed and experienced within its inverse and reverse. The writing offered the opportunity to represent a structure of feeling as it spiraled toward and away from the two of us. We were never at odds while dealing simultaneously with the odds—the oddity, strangeness, the engulfment that blurs and highlights into clarity and confusion. I loved coming in contact over and over again with my friend's brain-heart (Brenda). And I loved the invitation to allow a folding over and into and within, all the possible permutations of entanglement with another (Janice). If anything, the writing convinced us of the power of chaos. It was potent to let it rip, let the seams bust open, no holds barred. In this way, we conjured a mutual philosophic mandate of openness. Here, too, are shredded secrets blowing in the breezes.

Janice Lee (she/they) is a Korean American writer, teacher, spiritual scholar, and shamanic healer. She is the author of 7 books of fiction, creative nonfiction & poetry, most recently *Imagine a Death* (Texas Review Press, 2021) and *Separation Anxiety* (CLASH Books, 2022). An essay (co-authored with Jared Woodland) is featured in the recently released 4K restoration of *Sátántangó* (dir. Béla Tarr) from Arbelos Films. She currently lives in Portland, OR where she is the Operational Creative Director at Corporeal Writing and an Assistant Professor of Creative Writing at Portland State University. (http://janicel.com) Instagram/Twitter: @diddioz

Brenda Iijima is a poet, novelist, playwright, choreographer and visual artist. She is the author of nine books of poetry. Her involvements occur at the intersections and mutations of genre, mode, receptivity, and field of study. Her current work engages submerged and occluded histories, other-than-human modes of expression and telluric awareness in all forms. Her play, *Daily Life in China* is was published by elis press in 2022, and her novel *Presence* is forthcoming from Georgia Review Press in 2023. Iijima is the founding editor-publisher of Portable Press @ Yo-Yo Labs. She lives in Brooklyn.

A roundtable, unanimous dreamers chime in is a collection of vignettes of disintegration, mergers, and potentialities, a sensuous loosening of the human corporeal and psychic unit. Read Brenda Iijima's and Janice Lee's collaboration for the surge of energy that runs through this book's open pores. Enter a dizzying journey of an injured bike rider in an injured world finding new potentialities as a squirrel mistakes her for a tree, as she becomes squirrel, becomes tree, becomes parched by fire and cooled by river. "Trees are an interface," "the soil is a membrane," and the "I" fractures like a seed that needs the fire's heat to sprout. Walking humans, friends, strangers, a ritual for a dead small dog who might become a companion spirit: the stories reach toward connection in human-shaped and more-than-human shaped ways, allowing the feeling human 'I' to oscillate rather than vanish. Even the chance procedures of time and space conspire toward relation—"A list of the dog hairs that I didn't see but saved in my pocket." In this viral interspecies penetration, there's always searching: "Refugee status of microbes, pathogens—everyone looking for a home."

—Petra Kuppers, author of *Eco Soma*

This book reminds me that it is still possible to be astonished, like a book actually happened to me, language unearthed, heart brought back to life, storytelling as incantation, unbound cosmic song.

—Lidia Yuknavitch, author of *Thrust*

Matter is promiscuous in Iijima and Lee's *A roundtable, unanimous dreamers chime in*, leaking from one body to the next, creating an embodied syntax that communicates a meaning much wider, much greener and weirder than the one humans generally practice. One wants to lick this text. To digest and excrete it. This book is good soil.

—Sophie Strand, author of *The Flowering Wand*